'Kerry.'

He pressed the tip of his tongue against the pulse beating crazily in her throat. 'Do you have any idea how good you taste?'

His voice was low, slightly slurred.

And she wished he hadn't said that word. *Taste.* Right now, she wanted him to taste her. All over. She wanted him to explore her until she was quivering in need. She wanted his mouth to drive her right over the edge, and then some.

His hands slid further under her top, the tips of his fingers drawing patterns over her stomach. She drew in a shuddering breath, wanting more—wanting much, much more. And then he was cupping her breasts, his thumbs skating over the lace of her bra and creating the most exquisite friction against her nipples.

'Adam. We shouldn't…'

Immediately he dropped his hands. Pulled back. There was a slash of colour across his cheeks, she noticed, and his pupils were enormous, his cornflower blue irises narrowed to a fine ring round them. Right now, he was just as turned on as she was.

And he looked as shocked as she felt, too.

Kate Hardy lives on the outskirts of Norwich with her husband, two small children, a dog—and too many books to count! She wrote her first book at age six, when her parents gave her a typewriter for her birthday. She had the first of a series of sexy romances published at twenty-five, and swapped a job in marketing communications for freelance health journalism when her son was born, so she could spend more time with him. She's wanted to write for Harlequin Mills & Boon since she was twelve—and when she was pregnant with her daughter, her husband pointed out that writing Medical Romances™ would be the perfect way to combine her interest in health issues with her love of good stories. Now Kate has ventured into Modern Extra Romance, and SEEING STARS is her third novel for this series.

Kate is always delighted to hear from readers—do drop in to her website at www.katehardy.com

Recent titles by this author:

STRICTLY LEGAL
THE CINDERELLA PROJECT

SEEING STARS

BY
KATE HARDY

First published in Great Britain 2006
Harlequin Mills & Boon Limited,
Eton House, 18-24 Paradise Road, Richmond, Surrey TW9 1SR

© Kate Hardy 2006

ISBN-13: 978 0 263 84999 8
ISBN-10: 0 263 84999 6

Set in Times Roman 10½ on 12 pt
171-1006-58436

Printed and bound in Spain
by Litografia Rosés, S.A., Barcelona

SEEING STARS

For Maggie—
with thanks for the help on the Gaelic!

CHAPTER ONE

KERRY ignored the doorbell. It had to be a cold-caller, because all her friends knew this was her mega-busy time of year. She designed fireworks and displays all year round, but autumn was always the really crazy time. The time when she had to co-ordinate displays for Bonfire Night or New Year's Eve; the time when she had to sort out the computer detonation and design something even more exciting than the previous year's display. The time when people rang up at the last minute to see if she could just squeeze in a little something for them—oh, and could they have some music with it, too?

Right now, she was running on a good two hours' less sleep per night than she needed. And she absolutely refused to give up time on her pet project—developing a proper ocean-green firework, the holy grail of pyrotechnics. So tonight she really didn't want to have to stop what she was doing and listen to someone give a spiel about politics or changing her electricity supplier or what have you.

Buzz, buzz.

Go away, she mouthed. Who on earth sent out cold-callers at this time on a Friday night? Wasn't there a law against it? And the fact that she wasn't answering but her light was visible through the window, so she was clearly in…couldn't they take the hint?

Clearly not, because the doorbell kept ringing. In little short bursts. Insistently. And it was far worse than just one long ring because she couldn't tune it out. She *could* turn up the volume on her stereo and drown it out with Bach—but then she'd have her neighbours banging on her walls. With good reason.

Right. If this was someone who wanted her to change her perfectly good windows—or, worse, if this was her best friend, Trish, intent on making her stop work for now and dragging her to some boring party or other to meet her 'ideal man': a man Kerry didn't need because she was perfectly happy with her life as it was, thank you very much—she knew exactly where she was going to suggest putting the rocket she was working on.

She saved her file, marched to her front door and flung it open. *'What?'*

'Whoo. PMT. I knew I should've brought chocolate.' Adam leaned against the doorjamb, tipped his head on one side and gave her the full-wattage smile. The one that revealed his dimple. The one that made every female on the planet weak at the knees—including Kerry, because she hadn't quite become immune to it. Or to the mischievous twinkle in his blue eyes.

'Will this do instead?' He held up a bottle of very decent cabernet sauvignon.

She should've guessed it would be him. She folded her arms and tried to sound stern. 'What do you want, Adam?'

'A corkscrew and two glasses. But as we're in your flat, I'll play nice and let you choose the music.'

She rolled her eyes at him. 'Nobody's choosing any music. I'm working.'

He shook his head, adding another of the knee-buckling smiles. 'It's Friday night. Half past nine. Normal people don't work at this time of night.'

The comment stung, and she bit back, 'Your point being?'

'That you work too hard and you need a break. There is such a thing as work-life balance, you know.'

Now she knew he was teasing. 'Right. Says the man who works just as long hours as I do.'

He laughed. 'Yeah, but I play hard as well. That evens it out.'

Hard didn't even begin to describe how Adam played. He was the original party animal, who went snowboarding on his winter breaks and rock-climbing in the summer, and spent as many weekends as he could manage surfing the Atlantic rollers in Cornwall.

'C'mon, Kerry. You need a break and I'm supplying it. I'm even supplying the refreshments.' He nudged her gently aside and closed the front door behind him. 'Have you eaten yet?'

There were times when Kerry could cheerfully murder her upstairs neighbour. Usually at stupid o'clock in the morning when his current partner was moaning, 'Oh, *Adam*!' and Kerry's head was buried under three pillows so she couldn't hear his bedsprings creaking. And right now she really was busy.

But when he smiled at her like that, how could she resist him?

Adam McRae was lethal.

Worse still, he knew it.

She shrugged. 'I had a sandwich for lunch.'

'A sandwich? And lunchtime was a good eight hours ago. Kerry Francis, that's just not good enough.' He shook his head in mock-sorrow. 'What am I going to do with you? You need a properly balanced diet. I hate to think what sort of state your blood sugar's in. Sit down. I'll go and make you an omelette or something.'

'Your kitchen is upstairs. In your flat,' she reminded him.

'Yeah, but by the time I've brought an omelette downstairs and you've answered the door, it'll be cold and flat and disgusting. Much better for me to cook it here, when it'll be hot and fluffy and melt in your mouth. I take it you do have eggs that are within their use-by date? And maybe the odd leftover bit of cheese that hasn't gone completely hard?'

She waved her hands in a stop motion. God, Adam was such a whirlwind. He moved at a hundred miles an hour and expected everyone else to do the same. Heaven only knew how the nurses coped with him at work—then again, in the emergency department, Kerry supposed that you had to work that fast. 'I don't want an omelette, thank you. I'm fine. Really, Adam, I'm fine. I'm not that hungry.' She usually forgot to eat when she was concentrating, and by the time she remembered she was past being hungry. 'Will you please stop fussing?'

'Someone's got to look after you,' Adam said.

'That would be me,' she said, her voice cooling. She'd looked after herself for pretty much the last twenty years—since she'd first reached the age of double figures. That wasn't going to change any time soon.

'I mean properly, Kerry.' He ruffled her hair. 'Just sit down and make yourself comfortable, and I'll open this.'

He was telling her to sit down and make herself comfortable—in her own flat? Well, that was Adam. Bossy, organising everything. Probably force of habit from what he did all day long.

'I can't believe you've already run out of nurses to bother,' she said. 'You only moved hospitals a month ago. Surely you haven't gone through them all, already?'

'Oh, ha, ha.' He pulled a face at her and disappeared into her kitchen.

She followed him and watched while he retrieved two glasses from her cupboard and uncorked the wine. 'Seriously, Adam. You always have a date on Friday nights.' Usually with a different woman each time, although they all had a lot in common. Like having legs up to their armpits, stunning looks and long blonde hair.

So, so, *so* clichéd.

Which made it odd that Adam was here in her flat on a Friday night. OK, she had the long blonde hair—which she usually wore scraped up in a knot on the back of her head— but that was as far as it went. She had average-length legs and ordinary looks. And she definitely wasn't a Friday night companion for a tall, dark and handsome sex-god like Adam McRae. 'What's so different about tonight?' she asked.

He shrugged. 'I don't always go out on Fridays. Anyway, I was working a late shift today.'

Which meant nothing. She knew Adam could work a split shift and still party with the best of them, and be up bright-eyed and ready for an early shift in the emergency department the next morning. He was changing the subject to avoid the question—so something was definitely wrong.

Even though sometimes Adam irritated her beyond measure, Kerry liked him. Had liked him ever since the day she'd moved into the flat underneath his and managed to lock herself out, and he'd come to her rescue. Not only had he picked the lock to let her back in, he'd brought her a mug of coffee and shared a packet of chocolate biscuits with her. Definitely good neighbour material.

Over the last year or so, that relationship had deepened into friendship. A good friendship with no pressure. They understood each other. Adam was an emergency doctor who worked hard and played even harder, and Kerry was a pyrotechnician who preferred messing about with chemicals to socialising. They teased each other silly about their lifestyles but didn't try to change each other. If she was having a bad day, she'd knock on his door and he'd make her a latte, feed her chocolate biscuits and make her laugh. If he was having a bad day, he normally showed up at her door for a chat.

Like now.

So what was wrong? The obvious thing was also the most unlikely. Men like Adam didn't have women problems—unless you counted having so many women falling at his feet that he couldn't move. But she asked anyway. 'Women problems?'

'No.'

'Then what?'

'I just thought I'd call in and see my favourite pyromaniac.'

Kerry didn't bother correcting him to 'pyrotechnician'. He knew perfectly well what her job was. He just liked teasing her. 'Who happens to be working.'

'But it doesn't take you that long to design a rocket or even a whole display. You're brilliant at what you do—you could do it in your sleep. And yeah, yeah, I know you want to make the first ocean-green firework, but people have been working on the formula for years and years. Someone's not going to beat you to a chemical formula overnight, Kerry. You need to take time out—smell the roses, watch the clouds, listen to the birds.' Adam filled their glasses. 'Talking of which, do I get to choose the music?'

She groaned. 'If you mean you've brought some dinosaur rock with you, the answer's no.'

'Honey, it's the stuff to make fireworks to.' He batted his eyelashes at her and gave a mock leer.

'Not my kind of fireworks,' she teased back. 'For that, you need classical.'

He scoffed. 'What, "Bolero"?'

'What a cliché,' she said loftily. 'And, for your information, I hate Ravel. Try Rachmaninov's third piano concerto. About nine minutes into the first movement, and again almost five minutes later.'

'A double climax?' He looked interested. 'Oh, yeah? Where's the disc?'

'You can borrow it later. And you know perfectly well I didn't mean *that* sort of climax.' Typical guy. Everything revolved around sex, in Adam's world.

Though, now she thought of it...

No. She wasn't going to allow herself to think about sex with Adam. That would be way, way too stupid. It wasn't worth ruining a good friendship over sex. Even if the sex was spectacular—and she had a feeling that with Adam it *would* be spectacular.

'I meant my sort of fireworks,' she said primly.

Ha. It was sounding as if the lady did protest too much. She dragged her mind back onto a safer track. Work. 'Anyway, for a firework display you need something like Tchaikovsky's "1812", Handel...'

'No, no, no, no, no.' He wagged a finger at her. 'Think outside the box. You could do a really, really good show to some good old classic rock. Pink Floyd, Led Zeppelin, U2. It'd be fabulous.' That lethal twinkle again. 'Dare you.'

She shook her head. 'I'm not taking dares today.'

'Hmm. One day, I'll commission you to do me a show— to music of my choice.'

She laughed. 'You couldn't afford me.'

His eyes lit up. 'Oh, now that is most definitely a challenge.'

'No, it isn't. And you're beating around the bush. What's up?'

He looked faintly hurt. 'Do you really think I only come and see you when I'm out of sorts and need someone to talk to?'

'We-ell. No. Not always.' He sometimes came to see her

to tell her he was having a party and invited her to drop in if she wanted to. And they'd had dinner out together a few times—when he'd seen an ad for a new restaurant and wanted to try it out before he took one of his dates there. They were just friends. Good friends. Friends who gave each other plenty of space and could pick up where they left off.

He sighed. 'OK, just call me a selfish bastard.'

'You're forgetting "shallow" and "bossy" and "obsessed with sex",' Kerry said dryly. As well as charming and handsome and thoroughly good company, but she didn't think his ego needed stoking.

'Oh, thanks.'

'That's what friends are for.' That, and listening when their friends really needed to talk.

And if Adam needed to talk, he needed nibbles as well. And he'd been the one to mention food in the first place, so that probably meant he was hungry. Especially if he'd just got off shift—for all his moralising talk about eating properly, she knew full well he lived on chocolate bars and vending-machine coffee at work. Typical medic, who never listened to his own advice. She rummaged in the cupboard for a box of crackers, took some Brie and Dolcelatte from the fridge, dumped them on a plate with a knife, and shepherded him into her living room. She put the plate on the coffee table in front of the sofa, sat down next to him, then winced.

'Stiff?' Adam asked.

'No,' she fibbed.

'That's what you get for sitting at your computer for hours without taking proper breaks. Turn round.'

'Why?'

He rolled his eyes at her. 'Because I can't get the kinks out of your neck unless it's facing me. Turn round.'

Saying no to Adam when he had an idea in his head was

like trying to stop the tide coming in. It didn't work. Kerry went for the easy option and turned her back to him while he put their glasses and the wine bottle on the table.

'OK. Close your eyes.'

Lord, he had gorgeous hands. Simply gorgeous. And he knew exactly where to touch her. A blissful moan escaped her as he worked a particularly tough knot out of her neck.

Just for a moment, she imagined his hands touching her a little more intimately. Instead of working on her neck and shoulders through her T-shirt, he could be flattening his palms over her stomach. Sliding upwards to cup her breasts. Teasing the sensitive tips until she was tipping her head back and begging for more…

Uh.

Where had that come from?

Adam McRae was the last man on earth she'd have sex with. Firstly, he was her upstairs neighbour. If they had sex it would ruin their friendship, and she really didn't want things to get awkward or embarrassing between them—she didn't want to have to scurry down the garden path to avoid him. And secondly, she'd spent too much time living with a man like Adam. A man who had a string of girlfriends and thought only of his own pleasure and to hell with what anyone else needed. Been there, done that, knew better than to do it again.

She liked Adam—a lot. But no way would she get emotionally involved with him. It would be like lighting one of her special display rockets with a tiny, everyday household match: the whole thing would blow up in her face.

Painfully.

'Kerry? You've gone all tense on me.'

'Sorry.' She shifted out of his reach and cut herself a chunk of Brie. 'Thanks. I feel a lot better now.'

His expression said he didn't believe her, but to her relief he didn't push it.

He'd eaten half the crackers and the Brie had vanished completely before he told her what the problem was. 'My mum rang this afternoon.'

'Uh-huh.' Cue for a bit of self-pity on his part. As their only child, he was loved to bits by his parents. And Kerry knew he hated the feeling of being smothered. Ha. He should try having parents who didn't give a tinker's cuss. It might just teach him how lucky he was.

Not that she resented his luck, exactly. She just felt… empty, whenever she thought of her parents. *Ex*-parents: she'd heard of a case where a child had tried to divorce his parents, and she'd mentally divorced herself from hers. A long, long time ago. And she didn't need any replacements. She was doing just fine on her own.

'So what's wrong?' she asked. 'She wants you to spare them half a day out of the next year?'

Adam flinched. 'So you *do* think I'm a selfish bastard.'

Now she'd hurt him. Which she hadn't meant to do—thinking of her former family always made her want to lash out, and Adam had just happened to be in the way, this time. It wasn't his fault. She reached out and took his hand. Squeezed it briefly. 'Sorry. You might be right about the PMT. What's so bad about your mum ringing you?'

'It's my dad.' Adam sucked in a breath. 'Kerry… Right now, I need a friend.'

'Which is why you're sitting on my sofa,' she said softly. 'Talk to me.'

'He's had a heart attack. I'm not sure how bad things are.'

Adam worked in the emergency department, not the heart unit, but he was a qualified doctor. Which meant if he said something might be bad, he wasn't exaggerating or panicking. The situation really was serious. 'And you need to go back up to Scotland? Like now?'

'We were short-staffed so I couldn't go this afternoon, and I couldn't get a flight for tonight. I'm booked on the red-eye tomorrow morning.' Adam sighed. 'There's more. Dad—' He broke off, shaking his head. 'No. It's ridiculous.'

'Tell me.'

He sighed. 'You know I'm an only child.'

She nodded.

'So my parents see me as—well, I suppose, their future. Dad really wants me to settle down. Get married, produce grandchildren.'

'Which is about as likely as me making an ocean-green firework in the next two minutes.' She shook her head wryly. 'You think commitment means asking someone for a second date.'

He narrowed his eyes. 'I'm not that shallow, Kerry. I'm just not ready to settle down with one person for the rest of my life. I haven't met the one who makes me see fireworks with my eyes closed. I don't even know if she exists.' He sighed heavily. 'And I don't have time to wait until I find her. I don't know how long Dad has left. I'll have a better idea when I've seen his notes and grilled his consultant and can see for myself how he's doing, but it seems he's been having funny turns for the last year. Angina, probably. The fact Mum's kept it from me for months...' He shook his head in frustration. 'She's not the sort to pull a guilt trip on me. She's only telling me now because it's that serious. He could *die*, Kerry.' Anguish flickered across his face. 'He could die thinking that I'm a drifter and a disappointment to him.'

'Adam, I'm sure you're not a disappointment to your parents,' she reassured him. 'Look at you. You're a qualified doctor and you're good at your job. You're well on track to being a consultant, and you're still only thirty. You're doing just fine.'

'I don't mean professionally. I mean personally.' His face tightened. 'As I told you, they want to see me settled.'

Kerry had a feeling there was more to it than that. So she waited.

'They had this dream of me marrying the girl next door. Elspeth MacAllister. My parents and hers have been friends for years and years and years. Right from when we were still in our prams, they've been planning our wedding.'

And Adam liked to make his own choices. She could imagine just how he'd reacted to *that* idea.

'Don't get me wrong. She's a nice girl and I have a lot of respect for her.'

Which meant that Elspeth MacAllister wasn't a beautiful leggy blonde, Kerry interpreted silently.

'But she's really not for me. She'd hate living in London— she likes being in Inveraillie, with people she's known all her life. The sort of place where everyone's known not only you but your parents and your grandparents and…' He grimaced. 'That isn't what I want. I can't go back and settle down there, a place where everyone knows all of your business all of the time. Sure, I could get a job in Edinburgh, but I love my job here. I love London.' He drummed his fingers on his knee. 'I've been thinking about it all day. Dad needs to start taking things easy, but he won't listen to anyone who tells him that. I've tried suggesting before that he goes part time, does a four-day week instead of five to help get his stress levels down—he just scoffed and said it'd be more stressful trying to fit his work into four days instead of five. He deliberately missed the point.' He sighed. 'Mum's tried talking to him. But he just won't listen. So I was thinking, maybe I could make a deal with him. If he slows down, then I'll do what he wants and get settled.'

'What do you mean by "settled"?' Kerry asked.

'Engaged,' Adam explained.

'You can't get engaged just to please someone else!' Kerry protested, shocked. 'Adam, it's a crazy idea. It's not going to work. You can't handle dating the same woman for a whole week, let alone a real commitment like an engagement.'

'Not a *real* engagement,' Adam said. 'I'm not planning to get married. And it's not exactly to please him. I just need something that will make my dad slow down, for his health's sake—and this is the best thing I can think of.'

'A fake engagement.'

'A bargaining tool,' Adam corrected. 'Making a deal with him. Look, I know it sounds crazy, but we've tried everything else to get him to slow down. Maybe this will do the trick. He's so stubborn it probably won't work—though if it *does* work I'll need a fiancée.'

'Can't you just invent one?'

Adam shook his head. 'I'm a hopeless liar.'

That much was true. Adam might be able to charm the pants off women—and frequently did—but he never lied to them, Kerry knew. He always made it absolutely clear he was offering them fun for now, not true love for evermore. He was an outrageous flirt and a commitment-phobe, but he had integrity.

'My parents will want to meet her. So if my fiancée was invisible, it might be a slight problem.'

'There are only so many excuses you can make,' she agreed.

'Exactly. So I'll need a real fiancée on standby,' Adam said.

Kerry thought about it. 'That shouldn't be too difficult for you.'

He frowned. 'How do you mean?'

'Come on, you know hundreds of women.'

He shook his head. 'Not hundreds.'

'Lots, then,' She d exaggerated a tiny bit, but… 'Your little black book's enormous.'

He lifted one shoulder. 'That's as maybe, but nobody in my little black book would fit the bill. They'd all think me asking them to get engaged temporarily was a way of trying to save my face. To get married to them, without having to admit that that's what I really wanted to do all along.'

Kerry groaned. 'That's warped.'

'True, though.'

'How about a personal ad?' she suggested.

'It's hardly the sort of thing you can put in a personal ad.' He flapped a dismissive hand. 'Wanted: fake fiancée. Must be able to make my parents think I really love her and she really loves me. Mustn't get the wrong idea about me actually wanting to marry her.'

She grimaced. 'Put like that…yeah, you're right. Nobody's going to go for that. Not a personal ad, then.'

'There is someone who'd fit the bill,' he said slowly, looking strained. 'A friend.'

'Why don't you ask her?'

'She might say no.'

Kerry shrugged. 'You won't know until you ask her. And if you explain it properly and she cares about you, she'll help you out.'

'Good point.' The dimple reappeared briefly, and he took her hand. 'All right, then. Kerry Francis, will you get engaged to me—temporarily?'

CHAPTER TWO

'ARE you completely out of your mind?'

Adam blinked. 'Of course not.' She'd been the one to suggest it in the first place. *If you explain it properly and she cares about you, she'll help you out.* He and Kerry were friends. Good friends. He felt more comfortable around her than he did anyone else. He cared about her, and he was pretty sure she felt the same way about him. So maybe he just hadn't explained it properly. 'You're the obvious choice.'

'Like how?' she scoffed. 'You only ever date leggy blondes.'

He laughed. 'You have blonde hair.' Even though she kept it scrunched up in a knot at the back of her head, it was still blonde. Silky soft, he'd bet. Fine strands that would trickle through his fingers if he touched them.

Then he nodded at her jeans-clad legs. 'And, unless my anatomy tutor really led me up the garden path at med school, I believe those two things in your jeans are called legs…' Nice legs, too. Except she always kept them hidden under trousers. OK, her job meant clambering around fields and what have you, so jeans were practical—but he didn't think he'd ever actually seen her in a skirt or a dress. Even when they'd had dinner together somewhere, she'd worn smart trousers.

She glowered at him. 'That isn't what I meant, and you know it. You must be crazy. I can't possibly get engaged to you.'

A nasty thought occurred to him. Kerry didn't date that much—and she didn't date the same man more than twice in a row, either. He'd assumed that it was because she was dedicated to her career. Or maybe… 'Are you married already?' he asked quietly. He didn't think so—but if she was, she was probably separated and well on the way to a divorce.

'No. I just don't believe in marriage.'

That sounded a bit too heartfelt for his liking. Hmm. Maybe she was dedicated to her career precisely because she'd once been married or at least committed to someone and she'd been let down. Badly. And by asking her again, he'd dredged up bad memories for her. 'Kerry, I'm making a mess of this. But we're friends, right? Good friends.'

'Yes,' she admitted.

'I like you. A lot. And I've explained why I need a fiancée, so I can get my dad to take a bit more care of his health.' Adam raked a hand through his hair. Judging by the expression on Kerry's face, he was rapidly digging himself into a huge hole. She usually evaded talking about her background, so he was pretty sure there was something there that still hurt—but Kerry didn't tend to open up about her feelings, so he hadn't pushed her beyond her comfort zone. He'd kept things light between them. What you saw was what you got, kind of thing. If she wanted to talk, she'd talk.

'Look, I'm sorry if I'm dragging up bad things from the past by asking you to help me out here. But you're the best person I can think of to ask. You know I don't want to settle down. Neither do you—you're focused on your career. We both know exactly where we stand with each other. We're not looking for someone to be—I dunno—' he spread his hands '—*The One*. We both know that's a myth.'

Kerry said nothing, but took a large gulp of wine from her glass.

Oh, Lord. He really was making a mess of this. Which was crazy. At work, he always knew exactly what he was doing. He could judge a situation and start dealing with it in the most effective way, within seconds. How come he was blundering around so badly here?

'You're the only person I've talked to about this. The only person I *would* share it with, actually.' And in admitting it, he surprised himself. Kerry really was the only person he'd wanted to talk to about this. He'd been mulling it over all day at work. Whenever he'd thought of anyone else who might lend him an ear and give him some sensible advice, he'd just rejected them out of hand.

Because they weren't Kerry.

'Why?'

'Because…because I trust you, I suppose.' He shrugged. 'You and I, we're the same. What you see is what you get. No hidden agendas. I need help, Kerry, and you're the best person I can think of for the job.' He shrugged again. 'Dad's impossible so he probably won't go for the deal anyway. You'd be off the hook.'

'But if he does go for it?' she asked.

'Then I'm going to need to back up my promise. If I produce a fiancée out of nowhere, my parents are going to smell a rat—but they know about you.'

Kerry frowned. 'How?'

'You know they drive me crazy, fussing over me and smothering me and wanting to know every single detail of my life.' He grimaced. 'It's the way things are in Inveraillie. That's why I moved down to London, to get a life of my own without all the hassles and everyone knowing exactly what I'm doing every minute of the day. But it doesn't mean I don't love them, Kerry. I email them and call them a couple of times a week to see how they're doing. And my mum…' He smiled wryly. 'Well, she's good at getting information out of people.' She'd probably even be able to get Kerry to open up to her. 'I told her about you when you first moved in. She knows we've become friends. That you make a mean chilli and you drink red wine rather than white and you only listen to classical music.'

Kerry's brow creased even more. 'So how does that make me the most suitable contender for being engaged to you?'

'Because it's more plausible. We've known each other for a while. We get on well. And we've just discovered there's a spark between us.'

She still didn't look convinced.

Not that he could blame her. They'd never even kissed. Sure, they'd given each other a hug, and he'd given her a neck massage on several occasions, but it had been the touch of a friend, not a lover. They'd never been even close to naked together. When he was with Kerry, he didn't think about leaping on her and kissing her senseless. She was just Kerry, the girl next door.

Well, the girl downstairs, if you were being picky about it.

Being with Kerry wasn't like being with one of his girlfriends. It wasn't like being with anyone else in the world. Though, right now, he didn't want to analyse too closely how he felt in her company. There was a little red warning light flashing inside his head.

Not now.

He sighed and leaned back against the sofa. 'OK. Let me put it this way. Someone you never thought would ever settle down announces that he's going to get engaged. Are you more likely to believe him if he says it's a whirlwind romance

with a girl he met three days ago, or if he says he's finally
realised he's in love with someone he's known for ages and
wants to settle down with her?'

'Neither.'

He rolled his eyes. 'That's not playing by the rules. It's like
the shoot-shag-marry game. You have to choose. Either or.'

'Shoot-shag-marry?' Kerry asked, sounding mystified.

'Three famous people—you have to choose which of them
you'd shag, which you'd marry and which you'd shoot.'
He waved a dismissive hand. 'So which is most likely?
Whirlwind romance or someone he's known for ages?'

Kerry was silent for so long, Adam was about to prompt
her. And then she looked straight at him. Cool green eyes ap-
praised him. 'OK. You're right. It's more plausible if it's
someone he's known for ages.'

Good. She got the point. She was the perfect person for
the job. 'So will you help me? Please?'

She took another swig of wine. 'What exactly would it
involve?'

Well, that wasn't a straight no. He could work with this.
As long as he trod carefully. 'Whatever you feel comfortable with.'

'Meeting your parents and lying to their faces?' she suggested in a voice that just dripped with acid.

Time to backtrack. Fast. 'Maybe talking to them on the
phone. Telling them what you think about me.'

'What, that you're shallow?'

A tiny, tiny quirk at the corner of her mouth betrayed her.
She was teasing him.

At least, he thought she was.

He smiled back. 'If you want. Actually, once Mum had got
over the shock, she'd probably be pleased I'd met someone
who accepted me for who I am.'

The quirk disappeared. 'I don't like this, Adam. I don't tell lies.'

'Neither do I.'

'Then what do you call telling them that you're engaged to me?'

'The truth. Just not the whole truth—they don't need to know that it's all a fake.'

She shook her head. 'I can't do this. And how are you going to introduce me to them? "Hi, this is Kerry. She's the one who plays with explosives all day." That's really going to endear me to them. Not.'

He didn't see why she should be worried about what his parents thought about her job. She loved it, she was good at it…and it was a damn sight more interesting than working in an office or with dull, dull, dull figures. He was pretty sure he'd already told his mother that Kerry designed fireworks. 'Did I ever tell you that my mum's an art teacher?'

Kerry tilted her head to one side. 'And the relevance of this is?'

'Pigment. Colour. Arty stuff.' From the look on her face, she still didn't get it. 'You have things in common. Design and what have you,' he explained. 'You just happen to use different mediums. She works with watercolours, oils and pastels. You work with—' he risked a smile '—explosives and chemicals.'

'I'm not getting engaged to you, Adam. And I'm not going to lie to your parents for you.'

'Please, Kerry. I can't think of any other way round this.'

There was another of Kerry's long silences. This time, Adam waited. Knowing that she was thinking—and knowing that she thought fast. Maybe she'd come up with a different solution.

'Neither can I,' she admitted, at last.

'Then help me. Please. Just get engaged to me for a while.'

She set her glass down and drew her knees up to her chin, wrapping her arms round her legs. 'This is a business arrangement, right?'

'If you like.' He frowned. 'Do you want a legal contract?'

'No, a gentleman's agreement will do.'

Well, at least she trusted him. That was a good thing.

'And it's strictly for show.'

'Absolutely,' he agreed.

'So your parents will think you're settled and your dad will agree to start taking things easier.'

'Yeah.' But now he'd thought about something else. 'I can see what I get out of this. But what about you?'

She shrugged. 'How about polishing my halo and feeling good because I've helped a friend in need?'

'That's not enough.' She was doing something for him. He really should do something for her. And suddenly, he knew exactly what. 'I'll paint your flat for you.'

She blinked. 'You'll what?'

'You said when you moved in that you wanted to paint the place, have the walls something a bit brighter than magnolia.' He shrugged. 'It's been over a year now, and you still haven't done a thing.'

'I've been busy.'

'I know. So I'll do it for you.'

She shook her head. 'But you're busy, too. You work full time. Your job's demanding. You're a doctor, for goodness' sake. In probably the busiest place in a hospital.'

'And painting walls is about the best therapy I know after a rough shift.' He picked up on her expression immediately. 'And, before you ask, yes, I do know what I'm doing. I had a summer and Saturday job with the builder in our village. There won't be any drips in the gloss or missing patches in the emulsion.'

'You'll paint my flat,' she repeated slowly.

'Uh-huh. Think of it as helping you out, as a friend. Just like you're helping me out, as a friend.' He smiled at her. 'We'll go paint shopping at the weekend, or one evening when we're both free next week. You tell me what colour you want the rooms, and I'll do it.'

She shook her head. 'Adam, you really don't have to do that. I'll help you anyway.'

'Yeah, but you said it. That's what friends are for. Helping each other. You're doing something for me, so I want to do something for you.'

Kerry thought about it. Being engaged to Adam. OK, so it was all a fake—but even so word would get around that he was engaged, and the hordes of women would back off. She'd have a respite from having to stick her head under three pillows at stupid o'clock in the morning when Adam was…um…*entertaining*. She'd finally get her flat looking the way she'd wanted it to but hadn't had time to sort out for herself.

But she'd also have to be part of a family. Even though it was temporary. Something she'd sworn she'd never, ever do again.

She must need her head examining.

She looked at Adam. For once, he wasn't smiling. He looked tense, so tense that the lightest touch would shatter him into tiny pieces. Hardly surprising. That was how anyone would feel if they'd had the sort of news he'd had today. That his father was seriously ill.

Was she really hard-hearted enough to say no, she wouldn't help him?

Her parents would have just walked away. As they'd done with her, when she'd needed them most.

But she wasn't their child any more.

And she definitely wasn't going to behave the way they had. She'd do the right thing.

'OK. You're on.'

For a moment, he sagged in relief. Then he turned to her. Smiled. A warm, deep smile that really came from his heart. 'You are such a star, Kerry. Thank you. You've no idea how much this means to me.' To her shock, he pulled her into his arms. Hugged her.

And then he actually kissed her.

On the mouth.

It was the briefest of pecks, but every nerve-end in her lips seemed to be humming. Buzzing. Wanting a little more.

Wanting a lot more.

Oh, no. This was bad. She couldn't possibly start thinking like that about Adam. He might be her fiancé—as of a couple of seconds ago—but that was purely for show. They weren't lovers. Weren't ever going to be. There wasn't room in her life for a long-term relationship.

She opened her mouth to say his name, to say stop, to say this was a crazy idea and she'd changed her mind.

But then he gave her his little-boy-lost look.

Ah, hell. What could she do but go along with his mad scheme—even though she thought it would never work?

'I'm truly grateful,' he said softly. 'So when are you free, this week?'

'Free?' Uh-oh. He wasn't planning to get her to fly up to Scotland with him and meet his parents, was he?

'So we can go paint shopping,' he reminded her.

'Oh.' She walked over to her computer so he couldn't see the relief in her face, and flicked into her schedule. 'I've got a meeting Tuesday night. Otherwise, whenever you like.' That was one of the good things about being self-employed.

You could plan your own schedules, be more flexible than if you had to be in a certain place at a certain time every day.

Adam was flicking through his PDA. 'Thursday? And I'll shout you a curry afterwards.'

'OK. That'd be nice.'

'Right. I'll meet you back here after my shift.' He drained his glass and stood up. 'I'd better leave you in peace. Plus I've got an early flight tomorrow.'

'Sure.'

When he reached the door, she said, 'Adam?'

He paused with his hand still on the doorknob. 'Yes?'

'Let me know how things are with your dad, OK?'

'Sure. I'll call you tomorrow.'

He still hadn't left, she noticed. He was still standing there in her doorway, looking a bit puzzled—almost as if he'd just thought of something and wasn't sure how to tell her. 'Adam?'

'My parents are going to want to see a photo of you.'

She shrugged. 'Tell them you left it behind.'

Adam raised an eyebrow. 'In their world, people carry photographs in their wallet. You know, the kind you take in photo booths at railway stations.'

Just where was this going? 'And you want me to go to a train station with you at some ridiculous time in the morning, just to get a photograph?'

'Not at the kind of time I'll be catching the train to the airport. I'm not that mean.' He smiled. 'I was thinking of something a little easier than that.' He pulled his mobile phone out of his pocket. 'Smile?'

Well, he *would* have a camera on his mobile phone. Adam was a typical guy—loved gadgets, always had the latest model and always had the top of the range, so she'd bet the camera on his mobile phone would produce a pin-sharp image better than that taken by the average digital camera.

'Smile.'

She loathed having her photo taken. 'Is this really necessary?' she asked.

'Unless you want to fly up to Edinburgh with me tomorrow?'

She shook her head. 'No can do. Site meeting.' And even if she hadn't had the excuse of work, she wasn't prepared to meet the McRaes yet. Adam was an only child, so this engagement would probably be a big thing for his parents. They'd want to know all about her background—details she really wasn't ready to spill. And then maybe they'd welcome her as part of the family.

Except she didn't *do* families. Wasn't used to them. Couldn't remember the last time she'd felt part of one. Or even if she ever had.

'You're working. That's what I'll tell Mum, if she asks why you didn't come with me.'

'Yeah.'

'So smile,' he directed her. 'Smile as if whichever actor you've got a crush on has just walked into the room and asked you for a date.'

'Hmm.' Her favourite actor and Adam McRae certainly had a few things in common. Tall, dark and dimpled. Gorgeous. Charming. The kind of man who turned women's heads. She smiled, and he took the snap.

'Perfect,' he said. 'Goodnight, Kerry—and thanks.'

'No worries.'

Though as he closed the door, she began to wonder just which of them needed their head examining. This was never going to work. It was so obvious that it would all end in tears.

She just had to hope that their friendship would survive the wreckage.

CHAPTER THREE

ADAM finished reviewing his father's medical notes, and looked at him from the foot of the bed. 'I just wish you'd told me about your heart problems before,' he said.

'There was no point in worrying you, son,' Donald said.

Because he was too far away to make a difference? Did his parents really think he'd stay in London when his dad was ill and he was a qualified doctor who could make sure that Donald was being looked after properly? Adam shook his head in exasperation. 'Well, I'm worried now. Dad, you've got to take care of your health. It's important.' He paused. 'I think you should retire.'

'Oh, not that again.' Donald rolled his eyes.

'Come on, Dad. Face it,' Adam persisted. 'You're under too much stress. You've been saying for a while how being the headmaster means you spend most of your time in meetings and arguing over budgets. It isn't the job you love, any more. And if you carry on like this, you're not going to have a happy retirement with Mum. Because you won't be there to enjoy it.'

Donald scowled. 'You're exaggerating.'

'Am I, hell. You're under way too much stress, Dad. It's not good for you. Think about it. Do you really enjoy going to work in the morning, knowing that instead of running your school the way you want to you're going to be stuck in endless meetings with people who waffle and promise things they never deliver? And I don't care if your deputy's doing a good job—you're still under too much stress. Which is *not* good for your heart. Carry on like this—even part time—and you might not even see your next birthday, let alone retirement age. But if you retire now, take more exercise and take your medication properly, you'll be absolutely fine.'

Donald waved a dismissive hand at him. 'It's just a little blip, son.'

'Little blip?' Adam stared at his father in disbelief. 'Dad, you have angina. It's serious. And you clearly haven't been taking your medication properly, whatever you've told Mum. It's easy to forget, miss a tablet. Which turns to a couple of days' medication missed. And then a week's, because you've got out of the habit of taking the tablets.' He replaced the notes on the foot of the bed, folded his arms and glared at his father. 'Result, a heart attack. Which is why you're stuck here in a hospital bed right now.'

'It was only a little one,' Donald protested.

'*Only?* Dad, if you carry on the way you were before, you're heading for another one. A bigger one. And this time they might not be able to get you back again!' Adam shook his head and sighed. 'I wish you'd take me seriously.'

'I do, son.'

Adam resumed pacing up and down the room. 'I'll write the resignation letter and forge your signature myself, if I have to,' he threatened.

'Now you're being dramatic.'

'No. I want you to stay well. I want you to be around when your grandchildren arrive. I want them to know you and love you as I do. I want them to talk about the man who reads them incredible stories and teaches them the names of birds and how to hear the difference between their songs.'

'Grandchildren?' Donald scoffed. 'That'll be never, the way you're going. You've got a different girlfriend every week.'

Adam stopped pacing and looked at his father again. Donald had been the one to bring up the subject, so now was the right time to suggest the bargain. He just hoped this would work. 'I'll make a deal with you, Dad. You agree to retire and look after your health properly, and I'll settle down.'

Moira McRae walked in with two cups of coffee, heard Adam's last sentence and burst out laughing. 'Now, Adam. Fancy trying to make a bargain neither of you can fulfil.'

Adam knew his father wouldn't be able to resist the challenge. 'I will if he will.'

Just as he'd expected, his father perked up. 'All right. You're on,' Donald said.

Adam looked at his mother. 'Mum, you witnessed that. Dad agreed to retire and do what he's told, if I settle down. It's a deal. An unbreakable one.'

Moira rolled her eyes. 'As I said, neither of you will do it, so this is a pointless exercise.'

'Far from it. I'll type out his resignation letter on the computer when we get home tonight,' Adam said.

'Ah-ah.' Donald wagged a finger at him. 'You have to do your bit. And I don't mean when you're my age. I mean *now*. I'm not resigning until you settle down.'

Adam checked the machines wired up to his father, thought about telling him the news, and grimaced. His father really, really shouldn't have any excitement. He should be resting. Learning that his son was engaged could trigger another heart attack.

He really hadn't thought this through properly. Just rushed into it, the way he always did. Stupid. He didn't do this at work. He assessed a situation and worked swiftly, yes, but he did the right thing. In his personal life…he was making a real mess of it.

'See,' Donald said triumphantly. 'That look on your face— you know you can't do it. So the deal's off. I'm not retiring.'

'On the contrary,' Adam said. 'I'm just worried about whether telling you will give you another heart attack.'

'Telling us what?' Moira asked.

'That I'm…' Adam decided to take the risk '…I'm engaged.'

There was a dead silence.

Then, 'To whom?' Moira asked, sounding immensely suspicious.

'Kerry. My neighbour downstairs.'

Moira blinked. 'Kerry?'

Adam nodded.

'Isn't this a bit…well, quick?' Donald asked.

Adam had been prepared for that one. 'Hardly. I've known her for well over a year.'

'You never even told us you were seeing her,' Moira accused.

'I've been seeing her ever since she moved in. As a friend. Except recently I've realised what's right underneath my nose. The perfect woman.'

'Another one of your flighty blonde nurses,' Donald grumbled.

'No. I admit Kerry's got long blonde hair, but she normally wears it pulled back. And you know very well she's a py-rotechnician, not a medic. She designs fireworks.' Adam frowned. 'She's absolutely not flighty, Dad.'

'So she's a bit serious?' Moira asked. 'Too serious?'

'Sometimes. She's pretty dedicated to her job,' Adam admitted.

'You're telling us that you've chosen a serious, quiet girl, not a party animal?' Moira queried.

Adam winced. 'Mum, is your opinion of me really that low?'

'No, love. I just know you for what you are. A man who loves bright lights and the city and…I can't see you settling with someone who's not like that.'

Adam rolled his eyes. 'She lives in London, Mum. And I think fireworks qualify as bright lights.'

'Hmm. Is she a pretty girl?' Donald asked.

Adam smiled. 'Yeah.' And, to his surprise, he realised it was true. He'd never really thought about it before. But Kerry *was* pretty. Her eyes were sea-green and sparkling. When she was relaxed and laughing, her smile could light up a whole room.

But most of the time she kept herself at a distance from the people around her. He sometimes thought that if he hadn't rescued her on the day she'd locked herself out, she would have been the same with him. Polite, pleasant—and distant. Just the girl downstairs who'd smile hello if they came out of their front doors at the same time, but wouldn't choose to spend any time with him.

'Do you have a picture of her?' Moira asked.

'Um. Yes. But I can't show you right now.'

'Why not?' Donald asked, looking suspicious.

'Because it's on my mobile, and you're not allowed to use your mobile phones in the hospital,' Adam said. 'It interferes with the machinery. And considering how many things you're wired up to, Dad, that's a risk I'm not prepared to take.'

His parents both gave him a disbelieving look.

Adam sighed. 'OK. Mum, come with me into the corridor. I'll show you there.'

'What about me?' Donald asked, sounding pained.

'You're not going anywhere,' Moira informed him. 'I'll report back.'

As soon as they were out of earshot, Moira asked, 'You're not just saying this to make your father retire, are you?'

Yes. And trust his mother to pick up on it straight away. Kerry was right. This was a really stupid idea. 'No.'

'Hmm,' she said.

'I want him to retire, yes. I think it's the best thing for him to do. But I'm really engaged to Kerry.' Well, *nearly.* She'd agreed to do it if Adam's plan worked.

Adam flicked into the photos on his phone, and picked out the one he'd taken the previous evening. 'This is my fiancée.'

'I never thought I'd hear you say that. Neither did your father.' Moira studied the screen. 'Hmm. She's not what I expected. She looks more the girl-next-door type.'

Adam's mouth quirked. 'Strictly speaking, she's the girl downstairs.'

'Not funny, Adam.' Moira frowned. 'She doesn't look like your type at all. She isn't plastered in make-up, and although she's a blonde that hair's natural, not dyed.'

Ouch. Did he really go for that kind of stereotype? 'But you admit that she's pretty.'

'Yes. But much too natural to be one of *your* women.' She shook her head. 'No, you're not going to hoodwink me, Adam McRae. She might be your neighbour, but no way are you engaged to her.'

This wasn't how it was supposed to be. His parents were meant to be delighted, not suspicious. 'I'm not hoodwinking you, Mum. I really am engaged to her.' Except it was temporary. And he hadn't bought her a ring.

Yet.

'If you don't believe me, then I'll call her. You can talk to her.' Thank God he and Kerry had swapped mobile numbers ages ago—they were keyholders for the alarm in each other's flat. 'She's got a site meeting today about a big display she's sorting out, so I might have to leave a message on her voice-mail,' he warned.

'Hmm,' was all Moira said.

Adam speed-dialled Kerry's number. To his relief, she answered almost immediately.

'Hi, honey, it's me. I'm at the hospital in Edinburgh.'

Honey? Since when did Adam call her honey?

Kerry blinked in disbelief, and then the penny dropped. He was probably standing right next to his parents. Which meant that his mad scheme had worked and she was supposed to be his fiancée. 'Hi, Adam. How's your dad doing?'

'He's better than I was expecting. But I nearly gave my mum a heart attack when I told them about us.'

'So he agreed to take things easier if you got engaged?'

'Absolutely. I explained we were planning to come up together and tell them a bit later in the month, but we couldn't bring it forward to this weekend because you've got a site meeting.'

His parents were definitely there, she realised, and he was clearly doing his best to fill her in on the situation without giving the game away.

'We're in the corridor. Can't use the mobile on the ward,' he added.

So he was with just his mum. Who clearly didn't believe their story at all, or he wouldn't have called Kerry to back him up.

'And your mum wants to talk to me?' she asked.

'Yes.'

Oh, help. 'Adam, what am I going to say to her?'

'Girly stuff.'

'That's a *lot* of help,' she said, curling her lip. 'I don't think.'

'OK, honey. You're absolutely right. I'll hand you over to my mum.'

She was really going to have to think on her feet with this one.

'Hello, Mrs McRae?'

'Call me Moira, please. And you're Kerry.'

'Yes. Adam tells me his dad's on the mend. I'm so pleased to hear it.'

'Thank you, lass.' Moira paused. 'So you're getting married to my son.'

Not in a million years. 'Well, we haven't set a date for the wedding yet.' And they weren't going to, either.

'I see.'

Moira McRae didn't sound the slightest bit convinced. Kerry sighed inwardly. She'd have to make more of an effort.

'You've known each other a while,' Moira said.

Kerry chuckled. 'Yes. Since I moved downstairs and he broke in for me.'

'He broke in?'

Kerry recognised the sound of maternal panic and back-tracked swiftly. 'I'd locked myself out, and he rescued me,' she explained. 'And he also made me the best latte I've ever tasted. And fed me chocolate biscuits to help with the stress of locking myself out of my new flat before I'd even moved my things in.'

'I see. So that's when you fell in love with him?'

'I liked him right from the start, but love—no, that wasn't straight away. Adam lives life at a hundred miles an hour, and I just can't keep up with that. But when I got to know him better, I realised he only does it because he's scared he might actually be conventional at heart and *want* to settle down.'

'It sounds as if you know my son well,' Moira said dryly.

'I do. And he's a nice guy. Genuine. I have a lot of respect for him.' So far, so true. But Kerry knew that wasn't what Moira wanted to hear. Moira wanted to know if Kerry was in love with Adam. So she really, really had to act the part of the loving fiancée. Right now. 'I just thought of him as a friend. But then we were at this party and we ended up dancing together…and suddenly we just realised the spark was there between us. He kissed me, and it was like seeing fireworks.'

Kerry had the nastiest feeling that this might not all be made up. That if Adam ever did kiss her properly, it would be exactly like seeing fireworks.

'And you decided to get married.'

'You know Adam,' Kerry said. 'Whirlwind doesn't even begin to come into it. And once you've realised that you want to spend the rest of your life with someone, it's natural to want the rest of your life to start right then.'

'I know what you mean. It was like that when I met Donald. I'd known him for a while. And then one day I looked at him and saw who he really was—and I knew he was the man I was going to marry.'

Kerry would just bet that Moira had tears in her eyes right now, and hated herself for it. How could she lie to this poor woman—especially now, when her husband was lying in hospital and she needed all the comfort she could get?

'Welcome to the family, lass.'

Family? Oh, no. This was rapidly becoming more than she could handle. Please, please let Adam step in. Like now. 'Thank you,' she said carefully.

'Adam said you had business today, but I'll look forward to meeting you soon.'

'You, too,' Kerry said.

'I'll hand you back to Adam.'

If Kerry hadn't been sitting down, she would have slid to the floor in relief. 'Thanks.'

'Kerry? We're going back to see Dad, now. I'll call you tonight, honey.'

'Make an excuse—go to the loo or something,' Kerry said. 'I'm texting you now so you know what I've told her.'

'OK.' Sounding incredibly embarrassed, he added, 'Love you.'

When was the last time *she'd* said that, let alone meant it? But at least their conversation was private. She didn't have to say it back. 'I'll text you. Bye.'

She swiftly tapped in a brief resumé of her conversation with Moira.

If u add anything, let me know so we don't X wires.

A couple of minutes later, her phone beeped.
She scrolled down to the message.

U r a *STAR*. Thanx.

She smiled.

No worries. Delete txt in case ur mum sees it!

He answered almost immediately.

Good thinking. IOU.

Yeah. He owed her a lot. And she must be crazy, going along with this. Still, when Adam's dad was better, they'd be able to break their fake engagement very quietly. And nobody was going to get hurt.

'She seems a nice girl. Quietly spoken,' Moira said when Adam walked back into the little room. 'And she knows you well.'

'Told you so.' Adam acted nonchalant, but he had a nasty feeling he was just about to get a grilling.

'So when are we going to meet her?' Donald asked.

'Soon.' Oh, help. Kerry had warned him this would happen. He thought fast. 'This is her busy season. You know, planning fireworks. Bonfire Night, New Year's, that sort of thing. We'll sort something out.'

Please, please, let this be enough to keep his parents convinced.

'She's a pretty lass, from that photo,' Moira said. 'But nothing like your usual type. She doesn't seem like a party girl. Didn't sound like it, either.'

'She can party with the best of them.' Adam had his fingers crossed behind his back. Did Kerry go to parties? He really wasn't sure. She never talked about things like that to him.

'She said that's when you realised. When you were dancing together at a party.'

'Yeah. I never thought it would happen.'

'Neither did we,' Moira said.

Adam looked at both his parents and noticed an expression on their faces he'd never seen before. A kind of…relief. That he'd seen the light and was going to settle down. That they didn't have to worry about him so much.

Oh, Lord. He hadn't bargained on it working quite as well as this. OK, so he'd worked hard to convince them—and so had Kerry—but, to be honest, he really hadn't expected to pull it off. There had always been the chance his dad would refuse flat out. And when his parents had sounded so suspicious, he'd thought they'd see it was all a fake.

But now…his parents actually looked pleased. Happy.

'I always hoped you'd fall in love with young Elspeth,' Donald said. 'She's such a nice lass.'

'But she wasn't right for you,' Moira said. 'She wouldn't have settled in London. Whereas, as you said earlier, Kerry must like the bright lights, or she wouldn't be living there already.'

'Or do what she does for a living,' Donald added.

'So you're really settling down.' Moira smiled. 'I'm—well, I'll admit now I wasn't sure if you were just saying it to get your father to slow down. But now I've spoken to her… She sounds as if she knows you well. Loves you for who you are. And that's what I want for you. Someone who won't try to change you or make you miserable.'

'Just think, we're going to have a daughter,' Donald said, smiling at Moira.

Adam realised he'd been wrong about his parents. They weren't just *pleased.* They were ecstatic. He'd just given them the one thing they really wanted. A daughter-in-law. Hope for the future.

'And you mentioned grandchildren,' Moira added. 'You're really thinking about that?'

No, no, no! 'We don't *have* to get married, if that's what you're thinking,' Adam said hastily.

'Plenty of time,' Donald said with a smile. 'Children will come when they're ready.'

Uh-oh. It looked as if his father was already starting to count his grandchildren.

'And we'll look forward to meeting Kerry,' Moira said. 'Just as soon as we can.'

He smiled and nodded, outwardly relaxed, but inside his thoughts were racing. It sounded as if his fake engagement would have to become a real one. At least for a little while, until he could get his parents used to the idea that maybe he wasn't ready to settle down after all. Gently wean them away from the idea of him having a wife and children, so they weren't completely devastated by the news. And by then Donald would have retired and be living a less stressful life anyway.

Adam had made the deal. Successfully. But he had a feeling that it was going to be far more than he'd bargained for.

CHAPTER FOUR

On Monday evening, Kerry opened her front door to what looked like half a florist's shop.

'Hi, there.' Adam smiled at her over the top of the blooms. 'Can I come in?'

'Er, sure.' Why on earth was he carrying all those flowers?

As if he'd read her mind, he dumped them in her arms and said, 'For you.'

'For me?'

He grinned. 'Hey, can't a man buy his fiancée flowers? And as you happen to be my fiancée, as of Saturday morning...'

Not funny. She summoned up a smile. 'Thank you. They're very nice.' And what on earth was she going to do with them all?

The panic must have shown on her face, because he ruffled her hair. 'When was the last time someone bought you flowers, Kerry?'

She shrugged. 'No idea.' She'd always broken off her relationships before her men had got to the stage of giving flowers. And her friends usually bought her luxury chocolates, bath stuff, music or books for Christmas. She'd never bothered buying any flowers for herself—that would be a bit too sad. In fact, she wasn't even sure that she owned a vase.

'Well. This is my way of saying thank you. My dad's going to be out of hospital by the end of the week, and he's agreed to retire. Which is largely thanks to you.' He nodded at the flowers. 'These need to go in water, by the way.'

'Uh-huh.' What on earth was she going to put them in?

In the end, she used all her largest drinking glasses. The bouquet didn't look quite the same, split up like that, but she had to admit the flowers were pretty. And their scent was gorgeous.

'Next time,' Adam said mildly, 'I'll remember to get you a vase as well. Or buy you a hand-tied arrangement that comes with its own water supply.'

Next time? Kerry shuffled uncomfortably. He was intending to buy her flowers again? Uh-oh. This was beginning to sound like a relationship.

But it wasn't, she reminded herself. He was her friend, not her boyfriend. This engagement business was just to help him out until his dad had retired and was well again. She'd better not start getting too used to it. And besides, hadn't she always said she was best off on her own? She'd learned that in her teens. Nothing had changed.

She hated this kind of awkwardness. She covered it by pretending nothing was wrong—that they still had their old, easy friendship. 'Um, want a coffee?'

'Thought you'd never ask. I'll make it.'

She didn't bother protesting—Adam made superb coffee, so getting territorial with her kitchen would be spiting herself. 'I've got some *biscotti* somewhere.'

'Picked myself a fiancée in a million, didn't I?' he asked with a grin.

'Fake fiancée,' she reminded him, rummaging in her cupboards to find the Italian biscuits.

'You convinced my parents. And that's the main thing.' He

finished making the coffee, poured it into two mugs and handed her one.

'Cheers. Let's go and sit down.'

He followed her back into the living room and sat on the sofa next to her.

There were about six inches between them.

Weird how it felt too far away and too close, at the same time.

Ah, hell. She had to get a grip. She and Adam were *not* having a relationship. His women all looked like supermodels, and they lasted a maximum of two dates. Her dates…well, she was picky nowadays. She didn't go out with men very often. But they didn't tend to last more than two dates either. And she liked having Adam in her life. Having a relationship with him would be the quickest way to push him out of her life.

She cleared her throat. 'So are you back in Scotland next weekend, when your dad comes out of hospital?'

'Not quite. Best I can do is Monday morning. And I assume you're working?'

'Yes.' She could switch some things around, but she really wasn't ready to meet his parents yet. Especially as his dad was only just getting out of hospital.

'No problem.'

What would a real fiancée do in these circumstances? 'But I'll send a card and a get-well-soon gift with you, if that's OK.'

'I'm sure he'd love that,' Adam said.

'What kind of things does he read?'

'Anything and everything.'

She nodded. 'I'll see what the bookshop round the corner recommends.'

'You don't have to. But thanks anyway.' He smiled at her. 'Did you remember to get the paint charts while I was away?'

'Paint charts?' She looked at him, mystified.

'If we're buying paint on Thursday and painting on Friday,

you need to start thinking about what colour you want your walls. I assume you want to keep white ceilings?'

'Painting on Friday?' She stared at him. Since when had they agreed that? Yes, he'd said that he'd paint her flat. But he hadn't actually said *when*. 'Sorry, I can't. I've got a client meeting.'

Adam shrugged. 'I've got your spare key. I'll let myself in and make a start—you can join me when you get back.'

She frowned. 'Look, are you sure about this? You really don't have to.'

'I like painting,' he reassured her. 'Though I'm fussy about one thing.'

'What's that?'

'Music,' he said. 'I really, really, really can't work to Vivaldi or whatever this is you're playing.'

'Locatelli, actually.'

He rolled his eyes. 'Do you play stuff nobody's ever heard of on purpose?'

He thought she was practising one-upmanship? She laughed. 'No. When I was an undergraduate, one of the other students in my block of flats was reading music.' Her best friend, actually, but Trish and Adam had a mutual loathing society, so Kerry tried to avoid mentioning their names to each other. 'She let me borrow a few things. And I discovered I like this sort of thing.' Before that, she hadn't really listened to music much. She'd found a radio station that played really loud, really fast, tuneless stuff that her father—and a string of foster parents—had hated, and played it at full volume. But she hadn't actually listened to it. It had just been a convenient noise to keep people away from her.

Adam stared at her, the penny clearly dropping. 'Oh, no. You don't mean Trish Henderson?'

Said as if there were a very bad smell in the room. Which was exactly how Trish looked when she spoke Adam's name.

She sighed inwardly. 'Yes, I do. And she's still my best friend, before you say something you regret,' she reminded him.

'But she was just your neighbour, back then. I'm your neighbour now. So why don't you let me introduce you to rock music?' Adam asked.

'Because I happen to *like* this. And I'm not into the stuff you play.'

'Taking sides?'

Just what she'd hoped to avoid. 'Of course not.' Kerry folded her arms. 'Look, I know you two hate each other, and I have no idea why.'

Adam scowled. 'Because she's such a bloody diva.'

'She's a violinist. A very good violinist. And Trish is not a diva, Adam. She's one of the least pretentious people I know.'

He scoffed.

She frowned. 'Did she turn you down, or something?'

'No, because I've never asked her. Even if she wasn't married, she's not my type,' he said loftily.

Probably because Trish wore floaty ankle-length dresses and scarves, not high heels and miniskirts, Kerry thought. And she was brunette rather than blonde. And she seemed to be about the only female in the entire universe who was immune to Adam McRae's charm.

'You're missing out on an amazing experience,' Adam said.

Was he talking about music, or…?

Whoa. She needed to get her mind out of the gutter. Adam was confident, but he wasn't a boaster. He didn't really think of himself as a sex-god.

Did he?

She shook herself. 'I just prefer classical music.'

'One day,' Adam said, 'I'll persuade you to change your mind.'

'Mmm-hmm.' Kerry kept her voice carefully neutral. She

wasn't sure that she could cope with Adam in persuasive mode. Especially if any of that persuasiveness involved using that beautiful mouth on *her*…

Kerry got the paint charts the next day, and on Thursday night she met Adam outside their flats so he could drive them to the local DIY warehouse.

'I'm glad you've chosen something a bit braver than magnolia,' Adam said. 'Though yellow is almost as bad.'

'It's a good colour,' she protested. 'Sunny, bright.'

'But you've chosen a really pale shade,' he pointed out.

'I don't want anything too dramatic.'

He grinned. 'Yeah, I suppose you get enough of that in your job. Have you ever thought about having a firework mural painted specially for you?'

Kerry held both hands up in horror. 'Puh-lease. Don't be so tacky.'

He laughed. 'OK. Yellow in your living room, kitchen and bathroom, pale jade in your bedroom—mmm, actually, I rather like that.' He picked up a large can of the jade paint. 'I could almost be tempted to redecorate mine in this colour.'

'Oh, what? Your boudoir's more the sort Doris Day designed for Rock Hudson in *Pillow Talk*,' she scoffed.

He gave her a speaking look. 'You've never been in my bedroom.'

No, but at stupid o'clock in the morning Kerry knew just how Doris Day's character felt. Adam and Kerry didn't share a party line, unlike the characters in the film, but Adam's bedroom floor happened to be Kerry's bedroom ceiling…and she'd just *bet* his room was a love palace with switches by the bed to dim the lights and start sweet music playing.

He gave her a sidelong look. 'And, anyway, I don't date lots of women.'

Kerry snorted. 'By whose standards? Casanova's?'

He put his hand theatrically against his heart. 'Not now I'm a respectable fiancé,' he said.

She rolled her eyes. 'There's nothing even slightly respectable about you, Adam McRae.'

He laughed. 'That could be construed as a challenge.'

'Not when we're shopping for paint.'

'And the rest of it. Tut-tut. You can tell you've never decorated your place properly before.'

True. This was the first place she'd actually owned. The first place she'd dared to think of as home—because it was all *hers* and nobody was going to take it away from her.

Adam added a dazzling array of stuff to their trolley. Sugar soap, brush cleaner, sandpaper and masking tape, along with various brushes and rollers and dust sheets. 'Right, I think that should do us.'

It felt oddly domestic, pushing a trolley around a DIY warehouse with Adam. And when they went for a curry afterwards, as planned, it felt even stranger—almost like a date.

Except it wasn't a date. They were just friends. Adam wasn't going to hold her hand across the table, or play footsie with her under it, or kiss her goodnight at her door and leave her in a puddle of hormones, or sweep her up in his arms and carry her off to bed and make love with her until her head was filled with fireworks.

And just why did that leave her feeling hollow—disappointed, even?

When Kerry came back from her site meeting late on Friday morning, she wasn't really expecting Adam to be there—yes, he'd told her that he'd do the painting, and she knew he always kept his word, but on his days off she knew he always spent the morning in the gym or snowboarding on the dry ski slopes.

So when she unlocked her front door, the rock music blasting out came as a real surprise. Adam had swathed her living room in dust sheets—including her computer and filing cabinet, she noticed with relief—and was up a ladder, painting the ceiling.

A ladder that was presumably his, or one he'd borrowed from another neighbour. She didn't own one; she'd planned to use one of her kitchen chairs as a stopgap.

'Hi, there.'

Oh, Lord. He'd better not smile at her like that while she was standing on a chair. Her knees would turn to jelly and she'd fall off.

'Want a coffee?' she mumbled.

'Love one. I've nearly finished the ceiling, and then we can start on the walls.'

She glanced down at her clothes. OK, she'd been on a site meeting and had dressed for clambering around, but these jeans were newish. Businesslike. She didn't want to ruin them with paint. 'I'll stick the kettle on and get changed.'

This was crazy. Why was she feeling so unsettled? Maybe it was the fact someone else was in her space. Acting as if he belonged there.

But this was *Adam*. He often dropped in. It shouldn't feel like this. Shouldn't feel intimate. For goodness' sake, she'd seen him in snug jeans and a T-shirt plenty of times. He was easy on the eye—*very* easy on the eye—but she wasn't supposed to get that prickling at the base of her spine. Wasn't supposed to feel that tingling in her nipples. Wasn't supposed to want to brush her mouth lightly over his, tease him until the mischief in his eyes turned to passion and he tipped her onto her back and pushed his body deep inside hers.

'Get a grip. You are not going to have sex with Adam

McRae. This fiancée business is in name only,' she told herself savagely, and changed quickly into her oldest jeans and an even older T-shirt. A swig of coffee stopped the panic and made her able to act normally with him again.

'I'll put your coffee here, on the table.' Which he'd thoughtfully covered with another dust sheet.

'Cheers. Don't suppose you've got any more of those *biscotti* to go with it?' he asked hopefully.

'Someone not too far from here scoffed all of them the other night.'

'Oops. Sorry.'

Though he didn't look the slightest bit sorry.

He continued painting the ceiling, and Kerry couldn't take her eyes off him. He looked so cute when he was concentrating. The tip of his tongue was caught between white, even teeth. And, Lord, that body...

Crazy. She'd seen Adam in jeans that snug before. But she hadn't had this kind of view—where his washboard-flat abdomen was revealed as he stretched up, with a line of dark hair arrowing down into his jeans. Wow. No wonder women fell for him in droves. He could've been a model. Like the guy in the old jeans ad who stripped at the launderette and put his clothes in the washing machine and made every female heart in the place flutter.

She shook herself. Adam was off limits. And she needed to get back to the old teasing relationship between them—fast. 'You've missed a bit.'

'What?'

'You've missed a bit,' she repeated, pointing up to the corner.

He peered at the ceiling. 'No way. Where?'

She laughed. 'Gotcha.'

'Oh, for that...' He waved his paintbrush threateningly at her and started to descend the stepladder.

Kerry wasn't bothered: she knew it was an empty threat and he was only coming down because he wanted that mug of coffee.

So she was completely unprepared for the brush dabbed on the end of her nose. A brush full of white emulsion.

He'd just painted her nose.

She stared at him in shock. 'You… You…'

'Yes?' His blue eyes were just filled with mischief, daring her to react.

'Right.' She grabbed another paintbrush, dipped it in the emulsion and painted a stripe across his face. 'You asked for—'

She got no further, because he painted a corresponding stripe on her face.

The next thing she knew, they were both running round the living room, flicking paint at each other.

It ended when she was flat on the floor and Adam was pinning her down, waving his brush in triumph.

'Admit I won,' he said.

'No.' She wriggled one hand free and dabbed her brush on his T-shirt.

'I really don't think you should have done that…' His voice was full of laughter—and a threat. He was obviously planning to get his revenge. Messily. Involving a lot of paint.

Then he looked at her and his face changed.

He was going to kiss her. She just knew it. She could see it in the way his eyes had softened and his pupils had grown huge and dark. He was going to dip his head and brush his mouth against hers. Her lips had already parted in invitation. And every inch of her skin that was close to him tingled, from their tangled legs to her shoulders.

She could feel her breasts growing warm and heavy against the hardness of his chest. And it shocked her just how much she wanted him to slide his fingers underneath her

T-shirt and cup them. Rub the pads of his thumbs against her nipples. Lower his head and take one hard peak into his mouth.

Any second now…

He was going to kiss her. Wipe that teasing smile right off her face.

Even now Kerry's face was changing. Softening. Her habitual reserve was just melting away. And the way her lips had parted, inviting him just to dip his head and take his fill from her sweet, sweet mouth… Oh, it would be easy just to lean down and brush his mouth against hers until she was quivering. Nibble at her lower lip. Touch the tip of his tongue to hers and let the kiss heat up until her hands were fisted in his hair and his own hands were stripping away the barriers between them.

So they'd be skin to skin. Warm and soft and wanting. His thighs nudging between hers. Stoking their body heat, letting the temperature rise and rise.

And then he'd be inside her.

And—

No.

He shouldn't do this. Wasn't going to do this.

Kerry was his friend. He wasn't going to ruin one of the best relationships he'd ever had, just for sex.

The problem was, his body had other ideas. He was already hard, wanting her. All he had to do was tilt his hips and she'd know just how much he desired her. And he didn't think he was alone in this, either; he could see the pulse beating in her neck. Hard. Fast. Could feel her breasts swelling slightly against his chest. Could feel her nipples growing hard.

Ah, hell. He had to stop thinking about her nipples. How

much he wanted to touch them, taste them, watch the desire flare in her face.

He needed to put some space between them. Right now. Before this went too far. Before she realised just how turned on he was. Before it was too late for both of them.

'For that,' he said, levering himself off her and turning away from her so his erection wouldn't be visible, 'you can feed me.'

Ha. What he really wanted to feast on was Kerry's body. But if she read that in his eyes, he knew he'd be out of her flat faster than he could say 'sorry'. And right now he really wanted to stay close to her. Which meant playing nice and pretending that he didn't really want to take her to paradise and back.

Every single one of Kerry's nerve-ends wailed in disappointment when Adam moved.

He hadn't kissed her.

Hadn't touched her.

Which only served to prove how stupid she'd almost been. She'd been a hair's breadth away from reaching up, tangling her arms round his neck and drawing his mouth down to hers.

Thank God she hadn't.

Especially as his mind was clearly on food, not sex.

'Sure. I'll go and make us a sandwich,' Kerry said, hoping her voice sounded a hell of a lot brighter than she felt. If Adam had any idea that she'd actually *wanted* him to kiss her, it would be too, too humiliating. God. This was worse than adolescence, fancying someone who was so far out of her league it was untrue.

She had to remember that this fiancée business was for show. Not real. Adam didn't even find her remotely attractive—that much was obvious. Mortifyingly obvious. So she was going to be sensible. Keep their relationship the way it had always been.

Strictly platonic.

And ignore the little whimper inside her heart saying that it wasn't enough, any more.

CHAPTER FIVE

LATER that evening, Adam stood back and surveyed the room. 'It'll do,' he said, sounding rather less than convinced.

'I like it. It's clean and fresh and bright,' Kerry said.

'Yellow's still a boring colour.'

Kerry scoffed. 'Just because you go for bold and dramatic, it doesn't mean that everyone else has to.' Though it was yet another reason why his mother would never believe that they were engaged. Adam went for bright, fashionable shades to go with his ultra-modern furniture. She liked walls with a hint of colour and pastel-coloured, traditional sofas. Lots of cushions, soft lighting. They'd never be able to agree on a middle ground for a home together.

As if he'd guessed what she was thinking, he gave her a gentle nudge. 'Hey. We make a great team. If you get bored with fireworks, we could go into the interior design business. McRae and Francis.' He laughed. 'It's got kind of a nice ring to it.'

'Francis and McRae,' she corrected. 'Partnerships go in alpha order—like lemon and lime.'

'No way. There are loads of things not in alpha order.'

'Most of them are. Cheese and pickle, salt and vinegar, beef and horseradish,' she suggested, ticking them off on her fingers. 'If you want to go international, it's the same. Greek:

egg and lemon. Chinese: ginger and soy. Italian: basil and tomato. Loads of examples.'

'What about fish and chips?' he parried.

She shook her head. 'The exception that proves the rule.'

'I'll agree to disagree. For now,' he warned.

'What's the matter? Your competitive streak getting worried?'

He eyed the tin of paint. 'I could make you take that back.'

Kerry backed off. Fast. 'I'll make us some coffee.' She really didn't want to risk having another paint fight with Adam. Because if she ended up on the floor underneath him, she had a nasty feeling that this time he really *would* kiss her. Especially as her arms would be round his neck and pulling his mouth down to hers. She'd wiped most of the paint off her skin before she'd started making lunch, and Adam had done the same before they'd eaten, but there was still enough visible to remind her of what had almost happened.

What she really needed was a bath. But even thinking of that was a bad move, because she could just imagine Adam sharing the bath with her, soaping her body and teasing her until she was a quivering wreck...

Oh, get a grip, she told herself silently, and busied herself making coffee while he started to gather up the dust sheets. 'Um, shall I order us a pizza or something?'

Adam shook his head. 'Thanks, but I'm supposed to be somewhere tonight.'

Kerry reminded herself yet again that this fiancé thing was only for his parents' benefit, and it was none of her business what Adam was doing tonight. Whom he was seeing. Whom he was kissing. He'd spent a whole day preparing the surfaces for painting and then emulsioning the ceilings and the walls in her kitchen and living room and undercoating the glosswork. That was more than payback for a little play-acting. Why the hell would Adam want to ask her to go out with him tonight?

Just so he didn't think she'd been angling for an invitation, she said, 'Yeah, and I really need to go through my notes after this morning's site meeting.'

When they'd finished sorting out the dust sheets, Adam drained his coffee. 'See you later. Oh, by the way, do you mind if I call you from Scotland? My parents will probably want to talk to you.'

'No problem. Just warn me if there's anything in particular you want me to say to them.'

'Yeah. Thanks.' For a heart-stopping moment, she thought he was going to touch her. Hug her. Draw her close to him.

But then he smiled awkwardly, hefted the bag of dust sheets over his shoulder and left the flat.

And Kerry was left mourning their old, easy friendship. Before today, he would've hugged her. Ruffled her hair. Adam was the touchy-feely type and, although she usually kept people at arm's length, she'd rather liked him touching her.

It looked as if that was all over.

'Adam? Is something up?' Pansy asked.

Adam forced himself to smile. 'No, I'm fine. Just a bit tired. I might slip off in a minute, actually.'

Pansy stared at him. 'Are you sure you're OK? I mean, it's unheard of, you leaving a party before the end. You're always the last to leave.'

'It's been a busy week,' Adam said with a shrug. Though he knew what Pansy meant, and it unsettled him to realise that he was actually bored. Since when had he ever found parties boring? All those people to talk to and laugh with…

Except he couldn't get somebody else out of his head.

Somebody more softly spoken. Somebody who'd just hate the kind of music that was playing, drum and bass stuff with a throbbing beat. Somebody who most definitely wasn't a party animal, but somebody he could talk to all night—and then some.

'Hey. If you want an early night…' Pansy gave him a doe-eyed smile.

Adam recognised his cue. He was meant to put his arms round her, kiss her, and ask her if she'd like to come home with him tonight. It was what everyone expected of him. What he expected of himself, even. Pansy was his exact type: tall, leggy, blonde, pretty. So it shocked him even more when he found himself saying, 'Yeah, I think you're right. I should get an early night. I need some sleep. Catch you later.'

What on earth was wrong with him? He was passing up a definite offer. From a witty, pretty—no, *gorgeous*—nurse. He really must need his head examining.

All the same, he went to find his hosts, thanked them for a pleasant evening, and headed home.

Clunk.

Kerry glanced at her watch, and blinked in surprise. It was well before midnight. How come Adam was home already? When he was out partying, he was rarely back before two in the morning.

Give it half an hour, and she'd be hearing squeaky bed-springs and an, 'Oh, *Adam*!' she thought sourly.

Ah, hell. Why was she getting possessive over a man who wasn't actually committed to her—a man she knew wasn't even capable of commitment in the first place? Hadn't she learned anything at all when she was growing up?

'You need your head examining,' she told herself, and turned back to the chemical formula she was working on. And then she got up, grabbed her headphones and put on a

Beethoven symphony. Loudly. So when the bedsprings moment came, she wouldn't have to hear it. And wouldn't have to suppress the wish that it were her.

It was the Saturday morning from hell in the emergency department. Adam didn't manage to get a break until well past lunch. But as he sat in a corner of the canteen, he found his attention straying from his sandwich and coffee.

To Kerry.

And to the moment yesterday when their paint fight had turned physical. When he'd pinned her to the floor. When he'd stared into those beautiful sea-green eyes and realised how much he wanted to kiss her.

He'd *almost* bent his head and kissed her. Properly. Thankfully, his common sense had stopped him doing anything so stupid and ruining their friendship.

All the same, he couldn't help thinking about it. Funny how she'd said that to his mum about dancing with him and kissing at a party. If she'd been there at that party last night, it could easily have happened. And what would it be like when he kissed her?

He groaned aloud. Hell. He was even thinking *when* rather than *if*.

This isn't good, he told himself. Kerry Francis is not your fiancée for real. This is an engagement of convenience. In name only. She's just doing you a favour, as a friend.

Yeah, but you've stopped thinking about her in that way, haven't you? a little voice jeered in his head.

He tried to ignore it, even offered to step into the breach and do a split shift to keep himself busy, but it stuck with him all day. He had to face it. He'd stopped thinking about Kerry as his friend. And he'd started to think about her as a woman.

A very attractive woman.

A woman he wanted.

A woman he couldn't have: because she'd never, ever let him that close.

On Sunday morning, Adam's doorbell rang. He opened one eyelid the tiniest crack and glanced at the clock. Half past nine? What? And he'd intended to be out in the gym by nine this morning. This was crazy. He never slept in. OK, so he'd done a split shift last night, but he hadn't gone out afterwards. For the first time in a long while, he'd been in bed on a Saturday night before two a.m. And for the first time in a very long while, he'd been in bed *alone* on a Saturday night.

Cross with himself for sleeping in, he grabbed a pair of boxer shorts from the floor, pulled them on, ran down the stairs and opened the front door.

'Since when did you take to answering the door in just your underwear?' Kerry asked. 'Your way of silencing the cold-callers?'

She might sound sarcastic, but there was the teensiest flush on her cheeks. Interesting. So she wasn't quite as cool and calm as she liked to make out.

But she had a point. He was visible from the street wearing only his underwear. Probably not the best idea. 'Come in,' he said. 'Want a coffee?'

She shrugged. 'I wasn't planning to stay. Just dropping this off.' She handed him a neatly wrapped parcel and a card. 'For your dad. It's a book about Victorian Edinburgh.'

'Oh, thanks. He'll love that.' For a moment, Adam almost asked her if that was the sort of thing her dad read. Then he remembered: she'd once told him she'd grown up in an institution. She'd looked so wary that he hadn't pressed her to find out the whole story, he'd just assumed that her parents died in some sort of tragedy and she hadn't had an extended family to take her in. So asking her what her dad read would be way too insensitive.

And then it struck him. Kerry was a free spirit, with no family to crowd her. She had *space*—space to be whoever she wanted to be. The space he'd always wanted. And maybe he had what she'd always wanted: a family. Parents who'd taken an interest in what he did at school, who'd taught him to drive and taken him out to practise, who'd sent him good luck cards before every exam or interview and expected a call the second he had his results.

'I'll catch you later,' she said with a smile, and then she was gone.

Weird. She wasn't normally distant with him. Or did she think he'd got a girlfriend here and didn't want to play gooseberry?

He grabbed his mobile from the kitchen table and flicked through to her number. But before the line rang, he cut the call. If he told her that he didn't have anyone here, that of course he wasn't going to cheat on his fiancée, it would sound odd. Because she wasn't his real fiancée, was she? It was only a temporary arrangement until his father was better. And she wasn't in the slightest bit interested in his social life.

'Oh, what a tangled web we weave…' The words rolled unbidden into his mind. This little arrangement of theirs was already starting to get too complicated, and they'd barely even started. He was going to have to be careful. Very careful. Or the whole thing was going to turn into the most horrible mess.

'You OK, Kerry?' Trish asked as they walked through St James's Park.

'Mmm, just thinking about naked men.'

Trish burst out laughing. 'About time, too.'

Kerry frowned and stared at her best friend. 'What?'

'You, thinking about naked men.'

Kerry's jaw dropped. 'Oh, my God. Did I say that out loud?'

Trish grinned. 'Yep.'

Kerry glanced round her in alarm. Nobody was giving them funny looks—the tourists all seemed more interested in the water birds, thank goodness—so hopefully she'd got away with it.

'So what's his name, then?'

Oh, no. She wasn't getting into this conversation, even with her best friend. 'Nobody in particular.'

'C'mon, Kerry. You've definitely got someone in mind, because you're never distracted like this. Is he a client?'

Kerry shook her head. 'I never mix business and pleasure.'

'OK. Is he anyone I know?'

Yes, Kerry thought, but wild horses wouldn't drag it from me. ' No.'

Trish raised an eyebrow. 'Kerry, I've known you since you were nineteen and you always blush when you're bending the truth.'

Kerry sighed. 'Look, it's a bit…complicated.'

'Like how?'

She really wasn't going to get away with this, was she? 'His dad's seriously ill and the only thing he really wants is for his son to settle down and get married. So I'm a temporary fiancée.'

Trish looked pointedly at Kerry's left hand. 'So temporary that you don't even have a ring?'

'Er, yes.'

'And he's the one you're having naked-man thoughts about?'

Kerry's face burned. Put like that, it sounded…well, pathetic. She really needed to get a life.

Trish looked thoughtful. 'Does he know you feel this way about him?'

'No, and he's not going to,' Kerry added quickly. 'We're just friends.'

'Friends. And he has settling-down issues. Hmm. Obviously he asked you to do this fiancée thing because he thinks you're safe—you never let anyone close.'

Kerry scowled. 'I do. I let *you* close.'

'Yeah, but I'm female and I'm your best friend, so I'm not a threat to your lifestyle.' Trish sighed. 'Kerry, not all men are pondlife. Well, some are—like your neighbour.'

AKA her fake fiancé. Kerry winced. 'Why do you hate Adam so much?'

'I don't hate him. I don't even *think* of him,' Trish said loftily. 'I don't need to—he thinks enough of himself.'

'Oh, stop sniping.' Kerry waved a dismissive hand. 'He's all right.'

Trish shrugged. 'If you say so. The man who's left a trail of broken hearts all the way across London.'

'No, he hasn't,' Kerry corrected. 'He's always honest with his girlfriends and they know exactly where they stand right from the start.'

'You mean, a thousand miles from the aisle.'

'Exactly.'

Trish frowned. 'I'm just having a nasty thought. A seriously nasty thought. This fake fiancé of yours wouldn't happen to be a doctor, would he?'

Kerry didn't answer; she rubbed a hand over her face.

'Oh, no. Please tell me this doesn't mean what I think it does,' Trish begged.

'Look, we're just friends. And aren't you and I supposed to be having a nice, healthy walk instead of stuffing our faces with pasta, because you've decided you need to be svelte in case you pick up that award just before Christmas?'

Her hopes were in vain, because Trish didn't allow Kerry

to distract her. 'You're really playing with fire, Kerry. Adam McRae's more dangerous than a whole warehouseful of your flash powder.'

'No, it's fine. I'm not going to do anything stupid.'

Trish sighed. 'I just wish you could find someone like Pete.'

Trish's husband was a sweetheart—but Kerry didn't want the life Trish had chosen. She liked things the way they were. So the only person she had to rely on was herself.

'You need someone who'd support you and take care of you,' Trish said.

'I can take care of myself, thank you very much,' Kerry said stiffly. 'I'm very far from being a helpless female.'

'That's not what I meant. I meant mutual stuff, someone who'll be there when you need him—just as you'd support him if he was taking exams or going for a promotion or just having a rough time at work,' Trish explained. 'You can't rely on Adam.'

'I don't intend to. Though, for your information, he painted my flat on Friday.'

Trish frowned. 'That doesn't sound like him.'

'He's not all bad, Trish. Look at the way he came to my rescue when I moved in.'

'Hmm. If Pete and I hadn't been doing that week's recording with the quartet in Manchester—'

'Yeah, I know.' Kerry smiled at her. 'You offered to help, and you would've done if you'd been here and I probably wouldn't have locked myself out in the first place. But everything worked out OK in the end.'

'You're too independent, Kerry. What's that saying about no man being an island? You need to reach out to the rest of the human race.'

'I am,' Kerry protested. 'I'm walking through St James's Park with you right now, and I'm helping Adam with his parents. And I make people happy with my fireworks. That's enough for me.'

Trish said nothing, but Kerry could read it in her eyes: *so how come that last bit sounds so hollow?*

It was a question she really didn't want to answer.

CHAPTER SIX

TATTIES and neeps. Not alpha order.

Kerry looked at the text and laughed. She texted back.

It is if you do it in English. Potatoes and swede.

Two seconds later, her mobile phone rang. 'That's cheating,' Adam said plaintively.

'No, it's not. It's a fact. And if you're doing Scots pairings, there's porridge and raspberries. Which makes it two-one to me.'

'Hmm. Give me time.' He paused. 'I haven't disturbed you, have I?'

That depended on what you meant by *disturbed*. Kerry was beginning to think that Adam seriously disturbed her equilibrium. Why else had she had an X-rated dream about him last night—a dream that had left her hot and bothered when she woke? 'I was taking a break from work anyway.'

'Good. My dad wants a word, if that's OK?'

'Sure.' She suppressed the feeling of disappointment before it started. Of course Adam hadn't phoned just to talk to her. Had it not been for this fake engagement thing, he wouldn't have called her from Inveraillie at all.

'Kerry? Thank you for the book, lass. Very thoughtful of you,' Donald said.

'My pleasure. How are you feeling, Mr McRae?' she asked.

'Call me Donald, please. I'm doing fine. I don't know what all the fuss is about.'

'Adam bossing you around, is he?'

'"Trust me, I'm a doctor",' Donald mimicked, sounding thoroughly disgruntled. 'He's making a fuss about what I eat, what I drink—and he's told me I'm to take up golf. Golf!' He made a noise of contempt.

'Well, I suppose it's better than making you run up and down mountains,' Kerry said.

'But *golf*... Ach. And I can't even have a dram in the club-house, he says.' Donald sighed. 'Bossy. Just like his mother.'

All this teasing banter... Kerry couldn't remember it from her own home. Too long ago, maybe—or maybe her parents had never been like that in the first place.

'Is that Mozart I can hear in the background?' Donald asked.

'Yes. Piano sonata—'

'Number eleven,' Donald finished. 'Beautiful. I'm glad to hear my son has found someone with a decent taste in music.'

Kerry laughed. 'That's not what *he* thinks.'

'Aye, lass, but you and I know better.'

'Definitely.' To Kerry's shock, she found herself saying, 'My best friend's a violinist. If her quartet's performing in Edinburgh at some time in the next few months, I'll get tickets for you, if you like.'

'That'd be lovely, lass. And maybe you could join us. Doesn't matter if Adam's with you or not—we'd love to see you. So when are you coming up to see us?'

The question took her by surprise—she'd half expected it

from Adam's mother, but not from his father. 'Um, I'm a bit up to my eyes in displays at the moment. But soon,' she said.

'Maybe we'll come down to you, then. When my bossy-boots son says I'm fit to travel,' Donald suggested.

Oh, Lord. She and Adam definitely hadn't bargained on that one. 'That'd be lovely,' she said, hoping that the panic didn't show in her voice.

'I'll look forward to it,' Donald said. 'Bye, lass. It seems I have to rest. Doctor's orders,' he added in disgust.

Kerry chuckled. 'You take care of yourself.'

'And you.'

It was weird, watching his father talking to his fiancée, Adam thought. Kerry was definitely playing her part well; Donald was cracking jokes and in thoroughly good spirits.

But the weirdest thing was that Adam had felt the same when he'd talked to her. As if the world had just lit up. And that was crazy. Kerry was his *friend.* He shouldn't be thinking about her like that. He shouldn't be missing her. And he definitely shouldn't be remembering that almost-kiss and wondering what it would be like to kiss her properly. Wondering if she'd kiss him back.

Worse still, wondering *when* he'd kiss her.

'You look lost, son,' Donald said.

'Me? Oh, I'm fine,' Adam fibbed.

'Missing your girl?'

'Yeah.' He didn't have to play-act it: he really did miss Kerry. And that little fact scared him half to death.

Kerry replaced the receiver and leaned back in her chair. Ah, hell. She could easily fall in love with Adam's family. His dad liked the same music as she did, his mum could talk to her about colour and design, and they'd both welcomed her to the family. This was definitely going to end in tears. They really had to work out a way of letting his parents down gently. They seemed such nice people—the kind of parents she wished she'd had. People who deserved better than a pack of lies.

They needed to talk. Sooner, rather than later. She texted him swiftly.

Come down for dinner when you're back. Wednesday night, 7.30?

It took him the rest of the afternoon to answer. And then it was only a brief,

OK. I'll bring pudding.

At precisely seven-thirty on the Wednesday night, Kerry's doorbell buzzed.

'Hi.' Adam leaned against the doorjamb and smiled at her, holding a plastic carrier bag. 'Pudding. Which, I should say, is strawberries and cream. One point to me.'

She rolled her eyes. 'If you're doing fruit—apples and pears. Or bananas and custard. Which makes it two to me.'

'Bananas and custard? Oh, that is vile.' He pulled a face. 'I'm glad I brought pudding, if you think bananas and custard is…oh, yuck. That's a truly foul combination.'

'It's the best comfort food on the planet, I'll have you know. But it has to be proper custard made with eggs, cream and a vanilla pod—none of this add water to a packet mix stuff.' She closed the door behind him. 'Make yourself at home. How's your dad doing?'

'Getting there.' Adam put the strawberries and cream in her fridge.

He sniffed. 'Something smells nice.'

'Spanish pork. Should be ready in about ten minutes. Want a glass of wine?'

'Thanks.' He accepted a glass of red wine, and followed her back into the living room before making himself comfortable on the sofa. 'Don't suppose you feel like changing the music, do you?'

'No. This is soothing.' Mozart. Her favourite.

'Hmm. And that got you another gold star from Dad—he likes the music you listen to.'

'Which is probably why you hate it. You're still rebelling against your parents.' She laughed and joined him on the sofa. 'Most people grow out of that by the time they're thirty.'

'Yeah.' Adam didn't rise to the bait.

'He's not happy about you making him do golf, you know.'

'That isn't the only option. He needs to do some gentle exercise every day to strengthen his heart again. That's why I said golf—it's lots of walking, and there's a social side to it, too. Or he could get a dog and take it on a two-mile gentle walk every day.' Adam shook his head in disgust. 'Do you know what he said, when I told him he needed to do some exercise? He threatened to join the local squash club. He's just had a heart attack and he's thinking about a sport that's notorious for giving people heart attacks because they take it too fast!' His face tightened. 'My father is impossible.'

'You just don't know how lucky you are.' The words burst out before she could stop them. 'Your parents are lovely, Adam. They care—I mean, look at the way they've accepted me. A complete stranger. They've talked to me on the phone, they're interested in what I do.' The complete opposite of her own parents, who'd never really been interested in her even in the days when she'd lived with them. 'And they love you to bits.' He had two people who loved him unconditionally. A luxury she could only dream about. Why didn't he appreciate it?

Adam flinched. 'Sorry. I know you must have been only a kid when your parents died.'

She sucked in a breath. 'My parents aren't dead.'

'They're not?' He looked shocked.

'Well, not to my knowledge, anyway.' She had no idea where either of them was living now. And she wasn't in the slightest bit interested in finding out. Maybe once, but not any more. She'd moved on. To a place where she was happy.

He reached over and squeezed her hand. 'Want to talk about it?'

'It won't change things.'

'It might make you feel better, though.'

Would it? She wasn't so sure. More like it would be ripping off the protective plaster she'd kept over it all these years. But somehow she found herself telling him. 'My mother walked out on us when I was thirteen.' She couldn't meet Adam's eyes. 'My father had this string of bimbos. Probably worse than yours. She'd had enough of having to share him, and I can't say I blame her.'

'She didn't take you with her?'

Kerry shrugged. 'I think she'd had enough of being tied down, too. And she didn't know where she was going—the way she saw it, at least if I stayed with my father I was in familiar surroundings and I was settled at school, so there would be something constant in my life. If she took me with her, I could end up changing schools half a dozen times and having to settle in to half a dozen different towns. Maybe even abroad.'

'But?'

She shrugged again. 'As I said, my father had his string of bimbos. And I got fed up with him never noticing me. So I thought the only way to get his attention was to be as bad as I could be.'

'You?' Adam shook his head. 'No way were you a bad girl.'

'Oh, I was. I skipped classes, did no homework so I was always in detention, was rude to my teachers, and I was caught smoking time after time because I only ever smoked in places where I knew I'd definitely be seen. In the end I got expelled from school.' The head had called her father at work. He'd been absolutely furious with her. 'I thought I was being clever. But I played into my father's hands, because he sent me to boarding school. Out of sight, out of mind.'

'That's awful. I'm sorry. But I thought you…?'

'Grew up in care?' Kerry smiled mirthlessly. 'Yeah. I did. I hated boarding school. I thought if I got expelled from it, he'd realise how much I hated it and wouldn't send me back. So I acted up.'

'And he took you home?' Adam asked.

'No. He said he couldn't deal with me. He asked the social services lot to come and sort me out.' Her teeth gritted. 'He put me in care.'

Adam swore softly. 'How the hell could he do that to his own daughter?'

She'd asked herself that enough times. And finally she'd worked out the answer. 'Because I was in the way.'

'OK, so he was angry because you'd got expelled from a couple of schools. But surely he saw sense later, when he'd calmed down? Surely he realised why you'd done it and came back to get you?'

Kerry shook her head. 'I waited. For months, I waited for him or my mother to come and get me and say it had all been a stupid mistake.' To say sorry. To tell her they loved her. To say everything was going to be all right again. To say they were going to be a proper family.

It hadn't happened.

And she'd grown lonelier and lonelier. Tired of waiting.

'When I finally realised they weren't coming, I went off the rails a bit. I was fifteen, but I looked eighteen—so I drank, I smoked, I skipped school and hung about in shopping malls with other people who'd dropped out.' She sucked in a breath. 'Pushing the boundaries, I guess, to see how far I'd get before someone stopped me.' Except nobody had.

'Plenty of people make the same mistakes,' Adam said.

She laughed mirthlessly. 'Not on the scale I was making them, believe me. I went through three sets of foster parents in as many months. And I'd fallen in with a bad crowd.'

'So what happened?' Adam asked softly.

'I was moved to a children's home seventy miles away. The first lesson in my new school was chemistry. And the teacher was showing us what happens when you heat potassium permanganate.'

'Where it turns into a volcano,' Adam said.

Of course he'd know that. Being a medic, he'd done three science A levels. She nodded. 'I was fascinated. I skipped other lessons, but never chemistry. And then Miss Barnes—my chemistry teacher—called in at the children's home one Saturday and took me out to lunch. She had a long chat with me about my future; I was good at art as well as chemistry, so she suggested a career in pyrotechnics. I'd need qualifications in other subjects as well as chemistry, but she thought I was bright enough to catch up without too much of an effort, get good enough grades to do my A levels and then think about university.'

'So that's what you did?'

She shook her head. 'It gave me a sense of direction again, but I'd been messing about for too long to get away with it. I failed some of my exams, got low marks in others. Except art and chemistry.' She'd excelled, there. 'I wasn't going to bother going back to school, but Miss Barnes came to see me again. Made me realise that I had a choice: I could carry on the way I was and always be unhappy, or I could try again and put my past behind me. Rise above it. Succeed in spite of things. And she said something that's stayed with me ever since—the best revenge is living well.'

'You've done that, all right. You've made a name for yourself. And your name's going down in history as the one who developed the ocean-green firework.'

It took a while before his words sank in. Then it hit her. Adam believed in her. *Really* believed in her.

Which meant he was the only person apart from Miss Barnes and Trish who'd ever really believed in her.

Kerry wasn't sure whether it made her feel more elated or nervous. What he was suggesting was a huge amount to live up to—something she wasn't sure she could do. Her stomach was in knots and there was the biggest lump in her throat.

'Do you see your parents at all now?' he asked softly.

She swallowed hard. 'I suppose I could find them if I wanted to. But, the way I see it, they gave up on me over half my lifetime ago. I've got nothing in common with them any more. If they weren't interested then, why would they be interested now?'

'Maybe they've grown up,' Adam suggested.

Kerry shrugged. 'The sad thing is, I really don't care now. I'm past it. I don't need them any more. I'm doing just fine on my own.'

Before Adam could say anything else, the smoke alarm started beeping. With shock, Kerry realised what was going on. 'Oh, hell. I've just burned dinner.' She'd been so preoc-cupied with telling Adam about her past, she'd tuned out the scent of burnt food.

She rushed into the kitchen, took the pans off the heat, opened the kitchen window and flapped a tea towel underneath the smoke alarm until it stopped beeping.

And then she looked at the pans. The pork was beyond saving. The new potatoes had turned to mush, apart from the surfaces that had been in contact with the bottom of the pan, which were dark brown and hard.

What a mess. What a stupid, stupid mess she'd made of things.

Right now, she wanted nothing more than to howl her eyes out.

But she never, ever cried. She'd cried herself out as a teenager. Never again. She dug her nails into her palms, hard, and squeezed her eyes shut. No tears. Especially over something so stupid as burning dinner.

Adam walked into the kitchen. 'Anything I can do?'

'No, you're all right.'

Kerry sounded abrupt, and he smiled at her. 'Bringing your work home, hmm?' Then he saw the glimmer of tears in her eyes, tears she hastily blinked back. The abruptness had clearly been to hide how upset she was. 'Hey. I was teasing.'

'Yeah.'

She wasn't tearful over burning dinner—he knew Kerry didn't sweat the small stuff—but telling him about her parents had obviously got to her. Brought back all the old memories, the bad feelings. Ah, hell. He didn't want her to feel this unhappy. Not when he could do something about it.

He slid his arms round her and held her close. 'In a minute, you're going to wash your face, and I'm taking you out for a pizza.' He stroked her hair. 'I think you've done amazingly well, considering what your parents put you through. And what you've told me stays with me. I'm a doctor. Most of what I do is confidential. So I'm not going to gossip about you, or discuss you with anyone else, OK?'

She shuddered. 'Let me go. I'm being wet.'

'No. You're being brave and bottling it all up. When was the last time you had a good cry?'

'I'm not crying over *them*,' she said through gritted teeth. 'They're not worth it. And I don't believe in tears anyway.'

'OK. But just remember that tears aren't a sign of weakness. They're healing.' He moved just far enough away from her so he could see her face. 'As far as I'm concerned, what you told me doesn't change anything between you and me. Except maybe I admire you a bit more, because now I know just what you've had to deal with.' And he felt guilty, too: because he had the parents she deserved. The parents he didn't appreciate properly. He made a mental note to send his mother flowers in the morning, just because.

'You're doing just fine,' he said softly.

And then he couldn't help himself any more. He bent his head and kissed her.

CHAPTER SEVEN

ADAM'S mouth was soft, so sweet, nibbling at her lower lip. Teasing. Caressing. Even though Kerry knew this was the most utterly stupid thing she could do, she found her arms sliding round his neck and her mouth opening beneath his, letting him deepen the kiss. His hands had dropped down to cup her buttocks and he'd nudged her just that little bit closer to him.

Close enough for her to realise just how aroused he was.

But she knew this wasn't because of *her*. Wasn't there a saying that all cats were grey in the dark? And Adam had spent a few days in Scotland recently, in a tiny village where he couldn't even blow his nose without someone noticing. No doubt his parents had already told everyone he was engaged, so he'd obviously been starved of female company for a while. The only reason he was kissing her now was because she was female—and she was making herself available.

This had to stop.

Oh, Lord. But how hard it was, when his mouth had drawn away from hers again and was brushing a trail down the side of her neck. Tempting her. Inviting her. Inciting her. Making heat spring up wherever his mouth touched her.

All she could think of was Friday afternoon, when he'd pinned her to the rug and his eyes had gazed into hers. When her body had been aware of every inch of him. When her skin had burned and tingled and she'd wanted him to do exactly what he was doing now. Kissing her. Touching her—his hands had slid up to her waist again and his fingers had slipped just under the edge of her top.

Bare skin against bare skin.

This was getting dangerous. With Adam, she had a nasty feeling that making love would mean something. More than something. Something neither of them would be able to handle.

'Kerry.' He pressed the tip of his tongue against the pulse beating crazily in her throat. 'Do you have any idea how good you taste?'

His voice was low, slightly slurred.

And she wished he hadn't said that word. *Taste.* Right now, she wanted him to taste her. All over. She wanted him to explore her until she was quivering in need. She wanted his mouth to drive her right over the edge, and then some.

His hands slid further under her top, the tips of his fingers drawing patterns over her stomach. She drew in a shuddering breath, wanting more—wanting much, much more. And then he was cupping her breasts, his thumbs skating over the lace of her bra and creating the most exquisite friction against her nipples.

'Adam. We shouldn't…'

Immediately, he dropped his hands. Pulled back. There was a slash of colour across his cheeks, she noticed, and his pupils were enormous, his cornflower-blue irises narrowed to a fine ring round them. Right now, he was just as turned on as she was.

And he looked as shocked as she felt, too.

'I'm sorry,' he said, his voice soft and slightly husky. 'I didn't mean to take advantage of you.'

Who was he kidding? She'd been with him all the way.

'Better go and wash your face,' he said.

A breathing space. Exactly what they both needed. She smiled awkwardly at him and headed for the bathroom, knowing she was being a coward even as she did so.

The mirror told her it was worse than she'd thought. Her hair was all over the place—she couldn't even remember him taking the scrunchie out of her hair, and she definitely had no idea what he'd done with it. Her mouth looked as if it had just been kissed…extremely thoroughly. And her eyes glittered as if she had a fever.

Oh, this was bad.

She soaked a flannel in cold water and pressed it against her skin. Please, please let the coolness of the water do something to diffuse the heat Adam's mouth and hands had stoked in her. But all she could think of was the fact that if she hadn't said a word, if he hadn't stopped, they'd be in her bed now. Naked. Skin to skin. Exploring each other. Touching, tasting…

Oh, my. She started calculating chemical formulae in her head. Complicated ones. Anything to get her mind off the idea of sex—and especially off the idea of sex with Adam McRae. She couldn't go out and face him when her nipples were still showing through her T-shirt. When her tongue was practically hanging out. When her mind wasn't in control of her mouth and she was likely to beg him to take her to bed and to hell with the morning.

When she'd finally got her pulse back to something approaching normal and restored order to her hair and clothes, she returned to the kitchen. Adam had scraped the pans out and put them in soak. Cleared everything away. And he'd retuned her digital radio to a rock station, she noticed, not sure whether to be more amused or cross with him.

'Hey.' He smiled at her—and suddenly he was the old

Adam again. Her friend, her neighbour. Not the man who'd just kissed her until her temperature was rocketing. Not the man who'd looked at her as if he'd fasted for a month and she were a six-course gourmet dinner.

'Ready for that pizza?' he asked.

'As long as it's my bill. We're only going out because I burned dinner.'

'We all make mistakes,' he said softly.

Was this his way of telling her that what had happened between them was a mistake? Well, she already knew that.

'So we're having dinner *as friends*,' she clarified.

'Sure. By the way, a point to me—pizza and garlic bread.'

'Pizza and salad,' she retorted crisply. 'So that makes us even.'

'Peaches and cream.'

'Coffee and mints.'

'Oranges and lemons.'

'Fruit and nuts.'

By the time she'd grabbed her handbag and locked her front door behind them, she was five points ahead in the pairs game. And things felt almost normal…until they were sitting in the little trattoria, both of them reached out at the same time for a dough ball to dip into the melted butter, and their fingers touched.

A month ago, she wouldn't have thought anything of it.

Now, it made the blood fizz through her veins, and she couldn't look him in the eye.

This was stupid. A light, casual, accidental touch, and she'd gone up in flames. Part of her wanted to slide her foot out of her shoe and rub it up his calf, smile at him and let him know that she was happy for the spark to turn into a starburst. But she stopped herself at the last moment. She had to be crazy even to think about it—this was *Adam*. If they had sex, their relationship would be over by the morning. And, yes, although she'd like to have sex with him—right now, she'd like that very much indeed—she valued his friendship and didn't want to lose it.

Adam pretended to be browsing through the menu, but he was surreptitiously watching Kerry drink her wine. Lord, she had a beautiful mouth. And who would've thought she could kiss like that? He couldn't remember any woman ever making his blood heat so quickly. And the way her lips were pressed against the glass right now…oh, man. Just the sight was making him hard. He wanted to see her mouth parted like that, without the glass. He wanted her hair spread all over his pillow. He wanted her in his bed, wearing nothing but a smile. He wanted to drive her to the point where all the sounds she made were completely incoherent—to the point where that clever, capable brain turned to mush and she stopped thinking and just *felt* what was happening. Felt the heat between them.

But…

Hell, there was always a *but*. Kerry was his friend. Her friendship meant a great deal to him. He was more comfortable with her than with anyone else in the world, and he really didn't want to lose that feeling. Though if she had any idea what he was thinking right now, she'd run a mile and their relationship would be blown apart faster than one of her rockets.

He just had to keep himself under control. Resist the temptation.

Somehow they made it through dinner. Said goodnight outside their front doors. Adam kept himself under strict control and simply said the word instead of grabbing her, kissing her senseless and carrying her up the stairs to his flat. To his bed.

He was really glad that, for the next few days, work was crazy—and, thanks to being short-staffed, he ended up working double shifts. It meant he was too busy to think. And when he finished work, he spent his time at the gym or at the dry ski slopes, upping the intensity of his workouts so he didn't have the energy to think about Kerry.

Kerry, in turn, spent as much time as she could away from her flat; she needed to build and test fireworks, which meant working in a controlled environment. The lab was the perfect place to keep Adam out of her head—if she made a mistake with the fuel-oxidiser material or the chemical compounds she used to produce the colours of the fireworks, it could have disastrous consequences. Concentrating on them meant she wasn't able to think about him. And working long hours was the best way to avoid him.

It worked until Monday night—when she checked her mobile phone just before she headed home, and found a slew of messages from Adam.

Got a problem. Need your help. Please?

He'd sent the first one six hours ago. The rest of them were along the lines of 'please ring me as soon as you get this'.

It didn't sound good.

She scrolled through the directory to the number of his mobile phone. It rang twice, three times, and then was snatched up.

'Kerry? Thank God you called.'

It sounded so heartfelt, she went cold. 'Sorry, I only just picked up your message. I've been in the lab. Is your dad—' oh, please, please don't let it be bad, she begged silently '—all right?'

'Yes, he's fine.'

Relief pooled through her. She'd feared the worst.

'Um, do you have time to call in to my place tonight?'

She frowned. 'What's the problem?'

'Tell you when I see you.' He sounded distinctly uncomfortable. And Adam was the most relaxed, chilled-out person she knew. If his dad wasn't any worse, then what on earth had upset his equilibrium like this?

'What time?'

'Whenever you're free.'

She glanced at her watch. It was already getting late. 'I'm on my way back now.'

When Adam answered his door to her, half an hour later, she could hear classical music playing.

What? He only ever played dinosaur rock. She blinked. 'Am I having the hearing equivalent of hallucinations, or have you just had a taste transplant?'

'No.' He flushed. 'Just that I know you like this stuff. Want a coffee? Or maybe a glass of wine?'

If she didn't know better, she'd swear he was trying to butter her up. 'No, thanks. I'm fine. So what's the problem?'

'Come up.'

She followed him upstairs to his living room; he gestured to the sofa and she sat down.

'How's the testing going?'

'Great. I've developed a silver double helix starburst.'

'You can create a double helix? In the sky?' Adam looked intrigued. 'How?'

'Same way as you do any shaped burst. You put the chemicals in a binder to make a lump called a star, then mould the star into the shape you want. You can do heart-shaped ones as well. They're good for weddings.'

'Wow.'

She raised an eyebrow. 'I could yammer on about fire-works all night, but you didn't ask me here to talk about work. What's up?'

'My dad's a lot better,' Adam said.

'Well, that's good, isn't it?'

'Yes and no. Yes, because I can stop worrying about him now. No, because…' he blew out a breath '…my parents want to come down to London and meet you.'

So *that* was what this was about. 'When?'

'The weekend after next.'

So soon? She stared at him. 'And you said yes?'

'What else could I do? We had a good excuse for you not to join me in Scotland. But we don't have any real reason why they can't come here.' He cracked his knuckles. 'There's more. They want to stay with me.' He sighed. 'Well, of course they'll stay with me. They're my parents. I couldn't possibly expect them to get a hotel room.'

Well, obviously. 'I don't see what the problem is.' Apart from the fact that she was going to have to lie to them the weekend after next—and lie convincingly.

'These flats only have one bedroom. And my parents are going to have my room. But when my fiancée lives next door—well, downstairs—they're going to think it odd that I'll be sleeping on my couch. Which, I might add, is just a couch, not a proper sofa bed.'

She had a nasty feeling she knew exactly where this was going. 'So you'll be sleeping on your couch instead of with your fiancée, and therefore they'll realise that this whole thing was made up for their benefit.' She folded her arms. 'So what precisely are you suggesting, Adam?'

'That I sleep on your couch. Just while they're here.'

She hadn't shared her space with anyone in…she had no idea how long. When she was a student she'd shared a house with five other people, but since graduating she'd rented a variety of bedsits and small, single-person flats before she'd bought the flat below Adam's.

'I know it's a lot to ask.'

She sighed. 'Don't you think it'd be kinder if we told them the truth?'

'How can I do that? Look, Dad's a lot better, but he's not completely out of the woods. He had a small heart attack, Kerry, but there's a chance he could have another one in the next few weeks—a bigger one. I can't risk anything that's going to give him stress.'

'Isn't coming down to London stressful?'

Adam shook his head. 'It'll be four weeks after his heart attack. As long as he's OK to walk a hundred metres on the flat, he'll be medically fit to travel. And he's bursting to meet you, Kerry. So's my mum.'

'The longer this goes on, the worse it'll be when we finally come clean,' she warned.

'The longer we leave it, the longer it'll be since my dad's heart attack and the better his medical condition will be—so they'll cope with it a lot better,' Adam countered. 'So, can I stay with you? Please?'

She thought about it for a moment. Sharing her space with Adam. Adam, who used to be her friend but now she really wasn't sure how she felt about him. Whether it was lust or something even more dangerous. She should say no.

But she couldn't think of a single alternative.

She took a deep breath. 'OK. You can sleep on my couch. Which is a sofa bed, by the way.'

'Thanks.' He gave her that 'little boy lost' look again. The one that made her melt. 'We also need to get you an engagement ring.'

She shook her head. 'Now, that's really not necessary.'

They'd never planned this to be more than a fake engagement. They didn't need a ring.

He rolled his eyes. 'We're supposed to be engaged, Kerry. Which means you're supposed to wear a ring—that's what my parents will expect to see.'

'But a ring…I don't do jewellery, Adam.'

He'd noticed. She didn't need it. Or make-up—she had a natural beauty. One she kept hidden, most of the time. 'It doesn't have to be anything ostentatious. Just a ring. Whatever you'd like it to be.'

'Not an expensive rock. Something…subtle.'

'Your choice,' he promised. 'I'm picking them up at the airport a week on Saturday morning. So when are you free before then, to go shopping?'

She took her diary from her handbag and glanced through her schedule. 'Nothing I can't move, so I'll fit round your shifts. When's good for you?'

'Tuesday morning next week?' he suggested. 'I'm on a late. If we leave here at ten, we'll miss the rush hour and we'll still have plenty of time to choose a ring before I'm on duty.'

'Sure.' She scribbled a note in her diary. 'I'll, um, catch you later, then.'

Kerry wasn't sure whether to be more relieved or disappointed that he didn't try to persuade her to stay a bit longer. And although she'd worked out a dozen good reasons, over the next few days, why they shouldn't get a ring and he should tell his parents things hadn't worked out between them, when Tuesday morning came she couldn't voice a single one of them.

Because Adam smiled at her, took her hand and raised it to his lips, and whispered, 'Thank you.' The touch of his mouth against her skin drove all her common sense away.

Forty minutes later, they were in Hatton Garden, standing

outside an exclusive jeweller's shop. 'This is too much,' Kerry protested. 'I thought we agreed, no huge, expensive rocks? It's not as if it's a proper engagement. Can't we just—I dunno—use costume jewellery instead?'

He shook his head. 'It won't look right. Come on. I owe you one hell of a debt for doing this anyway. So just choose something you like.' He gave her a sidelong look. 'I wasn't planning on demanding it back afterwards. So you might as well have something you like and might wear, rather than something that would just sit in a box in a drawer.'

She glanced through the windows. There weren't any prices on the display. Which meant, if you had to ask, you couldn't afford it. This was way, way out of her depth. 'This stuff really isn't...it's just not me, Adam,' she said awkwardly.

He looked at her, his head tipped slightly on one side. 'OK. What would you be comfortable wearing?'

'Not a solitaire diamond. Nothing flashy.'

'Nothing like a starburst firework, then?'

She wasn't quite sure if he was teasing her or not. She shook her head. 'I think I'd prefer something...'

'A little less ordinary. Like you,' he said softly.

Yeah. She'd always been different, right from when she'd first become a bad girl. Even her choice of career was different. And it was just as well that this engagement was a fake, because she'd never fit into his family in a million years. She wouldn't fit into any family. Never had—even her own, completely dysfunctional one.

They wandered along the street, browsing in the windows. And then Adam stopped dead.

'Look at this.'

She stared at the deep blue cabochon stone with a white six-pointed star traced delicately across it.

'Almost like one of your fireworks. A starburst.' He glanced at the card beneath it, written in artistic script. 'It's a star sapphire.'

'It's beautiful,' she said, 'but maybe a little too big for me.'

Adam took her left hand. 'Mmm. You have small hands. A huge stone's going to look wrong. As a pendant, that'd work for you. But not as a ring.'

He ran his thumb and forefinger along the length of her ring finger, and heat pooled at the base of her spine. Oh, help. If she reacted that strongly to a light, impersonal touch, she'd—

No. She wasn't going to think about Adam touching her more intimately.

'What about that one?' He pointed to a green round-cut stone flanked by two smaller diamonds. 'It's exactly the same colour as your eyes.'

He'd noticed the colour of her eyes?

Oh-h-h.

If they'd been shopping for a real engagement ring, Kerry would've been melting by now.

'C'mon. Let's go see if it's your size.'

'Oh, the green sapphire?' the assistant said when Adam asked to see the ring. 'That's pretty.'

'I thought all sapphires were blue?' Kerry asked.

'No—they come in all sorts of colours. Any stone from the corundum family's a sapphire, actually—except red ones, which are rubies, and orange ones, which are padparadschas. You can get clear ones, but they're quite rare,' the assistant told them with a smile. 'Pink ones are very trendy, since they found new deposits in Madagascar.'

Adam laughed. 'No way would you wear something pink and girly!' He ruffled Kerry's hair. 'But the green one's lovely. It's really you.'

'Best way to see if you like it is to try it on. Do you know your ring size?' the assistant asked.

Hardly. She'd never worn a ring before. Kerry shook her head, and the assistant pulled a set of metal finger size rings from her pocket. She took Kerry's left hand and tried one of the rings. 'Hmm, too large.' She tried another, two sizes down. 'Perfect.' She took the ring from the display, and smiled. 'Well, that's a coincidence. It's your size. Must be fate.' She handed the box to Adam, who took it from the velvet casing and slid it onto Kerry's finger.

The ring finger of her left hand.

This was something she'd never thought would happen in her wildest dreams. She'd never intended to get married, or even engaged. And this wasn't a proper engagement anyway. But the way he was looking into her eyes as he slid the ring onto her finger… Lord. Her knees actually felt as though they were going to buckle.

'What do you think?' he asked softly.

The flanking diamonds caught the light, like tiny star-bursts. And the ring was an ocean-green—like the firework she so longed to develop.

'I…' There was a lump in her throat that just refused to let the words through.

'It has to be a green stone. Like your eyes. Like your dream,' he said softly.

So he'd picked up on that, too.

She just nodded, and hoped that the prick of tears she felt wasn't visible to him. Hell, what was it about Adam? Since this fiancée business had begun, she'd come closer to tears more often than she had in years.

'We'll take it,' Adam said.

She heard him chatting to the assistant and asking questions about the star sapphire, but she didn't register anything of what the assistant was saying. The only thing she could think about was what Adam had just said to her. *Has to be a green stone. Like your eyes. Like your dream.*

She just had to remind herself that this wasn't real.

And suppress the little voice in her head that said, *If only…*

CHAPTER EIGHT

TRISH grabbed Kerry's left hand and stared at the ring. 'Oh, my God. Please tell me this isn't what I think it is.'

'It's not for real,' Kerry reassured her. 'Just for show.'

Trish scoffed. 'This isn't costume jewellery, honey. This is the real thing. That's either white gold or platinum, and those are diamonds, not cubic zirconas. Please tell me you and that man aren't really…' she closed her eyes '…engaged.'

'No, of course not. But his parents are coming up next weekend and they'll expect me to be wearing a ring,' Kerry explained.

Trish opened her eyes again. 'Right. So it goes back to the shop afterwards.'

Kerry shook her head. 'Adam bought it for me. As a thank-you.'

Trish's eyes narrowed. 'A bunch of flowers or a box of chocolates is a thank-you. Maybe a pair of earrings or a bracelet, if it's a special thank-you—except you don't have pierced ears.'

Only because she'd let the holes close up. At one point Kerry had had four piercings in each ear and she'd seriously considered having her nose done, too. And her tongue. Something conspicuously outrageous. A badge warning people that she was a bad girl and they should stay away.

'A thank-you is definitely not jewellery like *this*—this is something else.' Trish grimaced. 'Please tell me you're not sleeping with him.'

'I'm not sleeping with him.' Kerry felt her face grow hot.

Trish groaned, clearly guessing the worst. 'But you want to. Kerry, you must be mad.'

Kerry held both hands up in protest. 'Hey, I didn't say I wanted to sleep with him.'

'You didn't have to—your face said it for you! OK. Do him, if you really have to. Sleep with him and get it out of your system. But, whatever you do, please don't fall in love with him,' Trish begged. 'It'll end in tears.'

Kerry already knew that. 'You're making a fuss over nothing. We're just friends. Look, I know you two loathe each other, but you have me in common, don't you?'

'Hmm.' Trish still didn't look happy. 'I worry about you, Kerry. What you're doing is—'

'Just helping a friend,' Kerry cut in. 'So will you stop worrying? Everything's going to be fine.'

Though Kerry felt a lot more apprehensive by Thursday evening. She tried to bury her nerves in work. And then her mobile phone beeped.

Victoria and Albert. Still OK 4 Sat? A.

Ha. She could do history, too. She texted back swiftly.

Elizabeth and Essex. Sat fine. What time plane in? K.

It was a while before he replied.

10.30 A.

So they'd be back here by lunchtime. Maybe, she thought, it would be easier to meet them on her own home turf.

I'll do lunch here then. K.

Her phone rang immediately. 'You don't have to do that. I don't expect you to put yourself out. You're already doing enough.'

'Adam, you're not going to have time to organise lunch before you go. It's no trouble. I'll do soup and salad so it won't matter if the plane's delayed.'

'Thank you.'

'Um, another thing. If you're going to be staying at mine, you'll need to bring some stuff down.' She paused. 'How long are your parents actually staying?'

'Not sure. We're leaving it flexible. See how Dad feels.'

There wasn't much she could say to that. But oh, it would be so much easier if she knew how long she'd have to keep up the pretence in public of being in love with him.

'When's convenient for me to drop my stuff off?'

'Whenever. Saturday morning before you go.'

'OK. I'll, um, see you then.'

Adam turned up on Saturday morning with an overnight bag, a vase and an armful of flowers. Pink ones.

'Girly,' she said with a grin. 'Are you trying to turn me girly?'

He laughed. 'I wouldn't stand a chance. But these'll go well with your kitchen—the colour contrast works perfectly.'

'Colour theory? Hmm. Teaching your grandmother to suck eggs?' she teased. Then smiled. 'Thank you. And for the vase. You really didn't need to.'

'Oh, yes, I did. Otherwise we'd be drinking juice out of mugs instead of glasses,' he teased back. 'Look, are you sure this isn't too much hassle, making lunch for my parents? I can take us out somewhere.'

'No, it's fine.' When she met the McRaes, she really wanted to be on her home territory. Somewhere she felt safe. Comfortable.

'Where do you want me to put this?' he asked, indicating his bag.

'My bedroom, for now.'

'So it's not cluttering up your living room, you mean.' He smiled. 'You know, I don't think I've ever met anyone as tidy as you.'

Yeah, well. When you never stayed anywhere very long, you learned to keep your possessions light. And tidy. Because then it didn't take long to pack. And she'd never quite got out of the habit.

She shrugged the thought away and busied herself arranging the flowers. And she nearly leapt a mile into the air when Adam's arms wrapped round her waist.

'Thank you,' he said, and kissed the exposed nape of her neck.

Spark to a starburst. Her whole body fizzed.

And then he let her go. 'I'll call you when I leave the airport,' he said.

'Uh-huh.' Kerry didn't quite trust herself to speak. What he'd done could be considered a friendly hug. Sort of. That kiss hadn't been a hot, wet kiss involving tongues. And he'd kept his hands outside her clothes. So why had it left her so hot and bothered? Why had it left her body quivering, wanting more?

'I take it that it's OK to use my key when I come in?'

She hadn't thought about that. If you had a key, you wouldn't ring your fiancée's doorbell, would you? 'Um, sure.'

He laughed. 'I've just thought. When I come in, I actually get to say, "Honey, I'm ho-ome."'

'Corny.' But probably what his parents would expect.

His parents.

Panic shot through her and she spun round to face him. 'Adam, how the hell are we going to carry this off? They're never going to believe that you and I—'

'Yes, they are.' He pressed his right forefinger against her lips. 'Just follow my lead.'

That scared her even more. Just what was he planning?

As if he'd read the panic in her face, he said softly, 'They'll expect us to do what any normal engaged couple do. Hold hands, maybe steal a hug or a kiss in the kitchen.' He traced the outline of her lips with his forefinger. 'We can do this. You've hugged me lots of times.'

Yeah, but not when she was wearing his engagement ring. A ring she hadn't taken off once since he'd put it on her finger. For the first day or two, it had felt strange. Now, it would feel a lot stranger if she took it off.

Which really, really wasn't good.

And a hug from a fiancé wasn't the same as a hug from a friend.

And a kiss… Oh, help. She didn't dare start thinking about kisses.

'It's going to be fine,' he said. 'Trust me.'

'Because you're a doctor?' she finished.

'Yeah.' He brushed his fingertip over her lower lip again; his eyes narrowed slightly, as if he were making a decision about something, and then he lowered his head and skimmed his mouth against hers, very lightly and very quickly. Her mouth tingled—in fact, her whole body was tingling, and she had the insane urge to step forward into his arms, slide her hands round his neck and yank his mouth back down to hers again.

Down, girl, she told her libido sharply. This isn't the time or the place. And he's not really your fiancé. He's just showing you how to act a part. Nothing more.

Though his eyes were very, very soft. And he brushed a tendril of hair from her eyes before saying, 'I'll call you from the airport.' His voice sounded odd. Husky. Sexy as hell.

Trish had warned her about this. Surely she wasn't stupid enough to fall for Adam? He wasn't serious about her. Wasn't serious about anyone. He'd only bought her flowers today because…well, because that was the sort of thing you were supposed to do for your fiancée. It was all just an act and he was warming up for the performance in front of his parents.

'See you later. Safe journey,' she said, and watched him walk out of her kitchen.

For the next few days—or however long his parents stayed—she was going to be sharing her flat with him. Separate rooms, admittedly: he was going to sleep on the sofa bed in her living room. But they'd still be sharing the same space. And sharing her space was way outside her comfort zone.

She finished arranging the flowers, prepared some soup and turned it down to a simmer, then made a space in her wardrobe to put Adam's things. Seeing his suit hung up next to her clothes sent a shiver through her. And putting his razor and toothbrush in her bathroom made her feel even jumpier.

She was going to be living with Adam. And if he kept touching her, the way he'd touched her and kissed her in her kitchen this morning, she had a nasty feeling that her common sense would be packing its bags and taking the first flight to Timbuktu.

It was going to be ages until Adam and his parents got back from the airport. And if she sat around waiting for them, doing nothing, she'd go crazy. She switched on her computer and settled down to working up a new display, co-ordinated to music.

The kitchen timer interrupted her briefly, reminding her to take the soup off the heat—she definitely didn't want a repeat of the evening she'd burned dinner for Adam—and she lost herself in work again until her phone shrilled.

'Hi, honey. We're on our way.'

'OK. See you later.'

'Love you,' he said quickly.

No, he didn't. That was play-acting, for his parents' benefit. Though the words still sent a thrill humming through her veins. *Love you.* When was the last time anyone had said that to her?

Oh, she really had to stop this. Right now. 'See you later,' she said, and hung up.

She had enough time to set her kitchen table, purée the soup and make a batch of blueberry muffins before she heard Adam's door close.

Well, of course he'd settle his parents in, first.

But time slowed down as if the second hand were moving through treacle. Lunch was ready, save for reheating the soup: good bread, cheese and ham on the table, a green salad, a bowl of tomatoes and a couple of deli salads she'd made herself to kill time. The kettle was full and ready to be boiled, and she'd put ground coffee in the cafétière.

Lord, Lord, Lord. If it was making her this nervous, meeting her fake fiancé's parents, how bad would it be if this were actually for real?

And then she heard the key turn in her lock.

'Honey, I'm home,' Adam called.

She wasn't sure whether she wanted to laugh or slap him. But she summoned a smile and walked out of the kitchen to greet him.

'Mum, Dad, this is Kerry,' he said. 'Kerry, these are my parents, Moira and Donald McRae.'

'Pleased to meet you,' Kerry said, holding her hand out politely.

Moira ignored her outstretched hand and enveloped her in a hug. 'So pleased to meet you, lass.'

Donald followed suit. 'You're even prettier than the picture Adam carries around on his phone.'

Adam *still* had that picture on his phone?

She tried her best to mask her surprise. 'Can I make you some coffee? Tea? Something cold?'

'Coffee would be lovely. If the doctor allows it.' Donald gave his son a baleful look.

'One cup,' Adam said. And sniffed. 'Kerry. Are those brownies I smell? Home-made double-chocolate brownies?' he asked hopefully.

'Muffins. Blueberry and raspberry.' She gave him an impish smile, and mouthed, Point to me. Then she turned back to Donald and Moira. 'Would you like to come through to the kitchen? I've made us a bit of lunch.'

'You've gone to a lot of trouble, lass,' Moira said.

'No worries. I would've made something like this anyway.' Just on a smaller scale.

'Muffins,' Adam said, and headed straight for the cooling rack.

'*After* your main course,' she said, tapping the back of his hand. 'You don't eat properly at work. You'll eat properly at home.'

Donald hooted. 'Perfect. You're getting a taste of your own medicine, now. You tell him, lass.' He handed her a box. 'Oh, and we brought you these.'

Hand-made chocolates.

Well, that was what parents did when they visited their grown-up children. Brought them something indulgent.

Ha. Her parents hadn't even remembered to buy her a

kiddy selection box at Christmas, when she was a child. Her dad had been too busy womanising and her mother had been too busy being angry about it. They'd never known her as an adult, and they weren't likely to, either.

She pushed the thoughts away. 'Thank you very much,' she said. On impulse, she hugged Adam's parents. 'I love chocolate.'

'Adam told us. And they're for you, so don't let him eat them all,' Moira added.

By the end of lunch, when Kerry had shepherded Adam and his parents into the living room while she cleared up in the kitchen, she wondered whatever she'd been nervous about. The McRaes were easy to talk to, showed an interest in her job— to the point where she'd even offered to take them to her next test run, to show them how a firework was put together—and they'd made her feel as if she'd always been part of their family.

Ah, hell.

She'd done something worse than fall in love with Adam. She'd fallen in love with his family. Right now, she really couldn't understand why Adam was so keen to distance himself from his parents. They *cared.* They wanted to know all about his job because they were proud of him, not because they were interfering. And they asked questions because they just wanted to be sure that he was happy. Why couldn't he see that? Why couldn't he realise just how lucky he was?

'Are you all right, lass?' Moira said, coming into the kitchen.

'Yes, I'm fine.'

'It's a bit daunting, meeting the in-laws for the first time. I'm sure Adam felt the same when he met your parents.'

Kerry bit her lip. 'I don't have any family, actually.'

'Oh, lass. Adam never said, or I wouldn't have been so tactless. I'm sorry. I didn't mean any hurt.' Moira hugged her. 'But you have a family, now. You have us.'

'Thank you.' Kerry blinked back the tears. That was just the point. From what she'd seen of them, the McRaes were the family she'd always wanted. But she wasn't going to get them, because she and Adam weren't really engaged. Adam wasn't ready to settle down—he might never be ready to settle down—so the happy-ever-after just wasn't going to happen.

She had to keep remembering that—or she'd be heading straight to heartbreak city.

'So this is the ring. Very pretty. And unusual,' Moira said, lifting Kerry's left hand and inspecting her ring.

'It's a green sapphire,' Kerry explained.

'The same colour as her eyes, Mum. And the colour of the firework that hasn't been developed yet—the one Kerry's going to create,' Adam said, joining them in the kitchen.

Moira frowned. 'I'm not with you. I mean, I know you have to work with different chemicals, in the same way that I work with different colour paints. But surely it's a question of looking at a spectrograph and working out which chemicals make that colour?'

'On paper, yes,' Kerry said. 'In practice, some of those compounds are extremely unstable—and some of them just don't work in nature. Ocean-green should happen if you mix barium and copper compounds with a chlorine producer—that way you'd get greeny-blue light emitted. But in practice, when you burn the barium compound it reacts with oxygen and hydrogen, so you end up with light emitted in the yellow-green part of the spectrum instead of blue-green. I suppose it's a bit like coloured glazes changing when pottery's in a kiln.'

Moira looked thoughtful. 'Of course—heat affects colour.'

Kerry grimaced. 'Sorry. I'm a bit in love with what I do. I tend to talk too much.' She shrugged. 'I have what you might call nerd tendencies.'

'Not at all. It's very interesting.' Moira smiled. 'And I'll really look forward to you showing us how you actually make fireworks. I've always loved watching the displays we have back home—especially the Hogmanay ones.'

'It's just as much fun putting it together,' Kerry said. 'Finding the right mix of different shapes and effects and colours to keep the audience interested.'

'And music,' Adam said, sliding his arms round her waist and pulling her back against him. 'Though she always sticks to classical. I keep telling her, she could do a fabulous show to rock music.' He nuzzled her neck. 'But she's so set in her ways.'

Oh, Lord. If he did that one more time, her knees were going to buckle. She couldn't help leaning back against him, and his hands tightened against her.

'I'm sending Dad back upstairs for a rest,' he said. 'Mum, why don't you go and sit down? Kerry and I will finish up here.'

Moira gave them a knowing look, as if to say she realised it was an excuse for the engaged couple to be on their own.

To Kerry's relief, Adam let go of her as soon as his mother left the room.

'You're impossible,' she whispered crossly.

'And you're fabulous.' He smiled at her.

Ah, hell. She couldn't remain annoyed with him for long. The mischief in his blue, blue eyes got to her every time.

But she was really, really getting nervous about tonight. About Adam staying over. Though it wasn't Adam she mistrusted.

It was herself.

CHAPTER NINE

THE rest of the day flew by. But after dinner out at the local Italian restaurant, Adam's parents retired to his flat for the night, and Adam and Kerry were left alone.

Adam sprawled on the sofa and smiled at her. 'You,' he said, 'were absolutely marvellous. My parents adore you.'

'They're lovely. And I hate the fact we're lying to them,' Kerry said. 'They really don't deserve this.'

Yeah. He knew that. He'd rushed into this whole engagement thing, and hadn't really thought it through. Now, it was obvious: from the second they'd met Kerry, his parents had loved her. She was sparky and bright and just the kind of daughter they'd always wanted. The kind they deserved.

But if he told them the truth now… He'd hurt them terribly. He sighed. 'Kerry, I can't come clean. Not yet. Not until Dad's completely recovered. He's doing well, but I can't risk a setback.' He tipped his head on one side. 'You really like them?'

'Yes. And you don't realise how bloody lucky you are,' Kerry said, 'having parents who are interested in you. Your mum doesn't ask questions so she can interfere in your life, you know. She's proud of you and she just wants to be part of your life because you're her son and she loves you. She just wants to be sure you're really happy.'

Guilt slammed into him. Kerry was right. Why hadn't he ever been able to see it that way before? 'OK. So I'm making a mess of my personal life. Take it as read that I'm sorry.' He grimaced. 'Can we drop the lecture, please?'

'Sure. Look, um, I'm a bit tired. So I could do with an early night.'

'OK. I'll stay up a bit later, if you don't mind. I'll try not to disturb you.'

'Problem, there. I'm sleeping on my sofa bed.'

He frowned. 'I thought that was where I was sleeping.'

'You're taller than I am. It's easier if I sleep there.'

She was suggesting that he should sleep in her bed? A rush of excitement flittered through him. *Sleeping in Kerry's bed.*

It would be better still if he shared it with her.

Though that was a problem. He'd been touching her all day. Little squeezes of his hand on hers. His mouth brushing lightly against hers. And that moment in the kitchen when he'd rested his hands round her waist and she'd leaned back against him... Not for long, but enough to make his pulse speed up. Enough to make him want to take her somewhere private and make love with her until neither of them could see straight.

He really shouldn't be thinking about Kerry like that.

And if he slept in her bed he'd be way too tempted to scoop her up and carry her there with him. Fan her hair over the pillow. Stroke her clothes away from her body and kiss every inch of skin as he uncovered it.

No, no, no. This wasn't what they'd agreed. 'Kerry, I'm not going to put you out like that.'

'But you're my guest.'

'I invited myself, so that doesn't count,' he told her. 'I've slept on people's floors plenty of times before now. The sofa bed will be fine. And then I won't be keeping you up, will I?'

'No, but it feels wrong.'

'We could—' The words were almost out of his mouth before he could stop them.

'What?'

If he said what he was thinking—that there was a third choice: sharing her double bed—she might throw him out there and then. In fact, there was no 'might' about it. She'd definitely throw him out there and then. 'Never mind. Look, I'm fine. Why don't I get my stuff while you're in the bathroom?'

'I… If that's what you want.'

It wasn't, but he knew she really wasn't ready to hear what he did want.

'Your stuff's through here.'

He followed her to her room, but couldn't see his bag anywhere. 'Er, Kerry? Where?'

'I put it away.' She opened the door to the floor-to-ceiling cupboard in her room. 'Your suit and shirts and gym stuff are in here.'

They were all neatly compartmentalised from her clothes, but they were sharing the same space. Which felt…weird. Nice weird, but still weird. As if they were a real couple, living together.

Something he'd never wanted to do with any of his former girlfriends.

But Kerry was different. She was his friend. His neighbour. Not girlfriend material.

So why couldn't he stop himself wondering how it would be between them if this were for real? Why did he actually like the fact that her things were together with his?

'And I cleared out the top drawer for the rest of your stuff.' She gestured towards the pine chest of drawers at the foot of her bed. 'Your shaving things are in the bathroom.'

'Thanks.' He smiled at her. 'You're so organised.'

'And there's a problem with that?'

She sounded slightly defensive and prickly, and Adam could have kicked himself. He hadn't been criticising. 'No, it's refreshing. I spend my days in chaos. It's nice not to be in chaos at home.'

Then he realised what he'd just said. *Home.* The strange thing was, he felt comfortable here, even though Kerry's taste wasn't the same as his. He had a nasty suspicion that this place felt like home to him just because she was there. Cool and calm and practical and organised. Kerry Francis was someone you could rely on. He came to her when he'd had a rough shift, because he always felt better around her. And he always tried out new restaurants with her because he didn't have to make scintillating conversation or impress anyone, he could just be himself and she accepted him for what he was.

Now he thought about it, apart from his mother, Kerry was about the only constant female in his life.

Ah, hell. She was his friend, not his lover.

But an insidious voice in his head asked, *Why can't she be both?*

He knew the answer to that one. Because he wasn't ready to settle down. She didn't want to settle down, either. And if he told Kerry that he was starting to fall for her, she'd put a barrier straight up between them. Block him out of her life.

He didn't want that to happen.

So he was going to have to play this very, very carefully. Keep himself under strict control. 'Thanks for putting me up,' he said softly.

'No problem. I'll go and make up the sofa bed.'

He shook his head. 'You're tired. I'll sort it out. Just point me in the right direction for pillows and what have you.'

She gestured to the shelves above the wardrobe space. 'Pillows, spare duvet, bed-linen. Help yourself.'

'Cheers.'

He'd just finished making up the sofa bed when she came out of the bathroom. She was wearing pyjamas and a thick, fluffy towelling dressing gown belted tightly round her. About the only naked skin visible was on her throat and her feet. She had pretty feet, he noticed. No nail polish, no toe rings, just bare, soft, smooth feet. And as for her throat…

No. He wasn't going to dwell on that, because his self-control was in severe danger of snapping. 'Goodnight,' he said. 'Sleep well.'

'You, too.'

He didn't think he would, somehow. He was too aware of the woman in the next room to him. And even more aware of the fact that his feelings towards her had changed.

He was falling for her. For the first time ever, Adam realised he was falling in love. Worse, he was falling in love with a woman who most definitely didn't *do* love. A woman who was more self-contained than any he'd ever met. A woman with a past that made her wary of people.

So how was he going to get her to change her mind? More specifically: how was he going to get her to change her mind about him, and see him as more than just the guy upstairs?

Adam didn't have any answers by seven o'clock the following morning. But he was wide awake and stir crazy. He knew the best thing he could do when he was in this sort of mood was to hit the gym—hard. The problem was, his gym stuff was in Kerry's bedroom.

He *could* tiptoe in and try to retrieve it without waking her. And then she'd be embarrassed. No, there was a better way. He made her a mug of coffee, just the way he knew she liked it, then knocked lightly on her door. 'Kerry?'

No answer.

He knocked again and then opened the door slightly. 'Kerry?'

'Huh?' She jackknifed up. 'Adam?'

'I brought you a coffee.' He pushed the door open wider. The light from the living room showed that she'd sat up without pulling the duvet with her to cover herself. Her pyjama top was camisole-style with a v-shaped neckline and little spaghetti straps. And there were little hearts scattered all over it. Pretty, feminine—so unlike the workmanlike way she usually dressed. Jeans for a site visit or lab work, smart trousers for a client meeting or dinner out with him. Why did she hide this side of herself—the soft, frilly, girly side?

He put the mug of coffee on her bedside cabinet, then sat down on the side of her bed.

'Sleep well?'

She nodded. 'You?'

'Mmm.' Lord, she looked lovely with her hair down like that. All mussed and…wanton. Her eyes were soft and sleepy, and her mouth was so incredibly sexy.

The evening when he'd kissed her and slid his hands under her top, he'd cupped her breasts over her bra. This time, there wouldn't be any material between him and her skin. All he had to do was lean over. Brush his mouth against hers, tease her until the spark lit between them and she kissed him back. Touch her the way he was aching to touch her. Push that pretty little camisole up and up and up until she was bared to his view. So he could see her. Touch her. Taste her.

He was even swaying towards her when he realised what he was doing.

No. She wasn't ready for this. And he didn't want to ruin things between them before they'd even started.

'Is it OK if I get my gym stuff from your wardrobe?' he asked.

'Uh, sure.'

Was she staring at his mouth as if she were desperate for it to be glued to hers, or was he just seeing what he wanted to see?

He didn't take the risk. He simply smiled and edged off her bed again, before he did something stupid. Like climbing in beside her and sliding those little straps off her shoulders, kissing every inch of skin he'd bared, and then pushing the material down to reveal her breasts.

Like telling her how hot she made him feel.

Like making crazy, passionate love to her until they were both seeing starbursts.

'I thought I'd have a workout first thing,' he said, fishing his running shoes, T-shirt and shorts from her wardrobe. 'Mum and Dad'll be awake by the time I get back, so I'll go straight up. I was going to take them out for a drive, have lunch in a pub somewhere. Want to come with us?'

Tempting. So very tempting. A day spent with Adam and his family. A lazy Sunday. The kind of day that Kerry had always labelled as being in her dreams and not to be wished for because it wasn't going to happen.

She couldn't do it. Dared not do it. Because if she did it once, she'd want to do it again. And again.

She was already halfway to falling in love with Adam—and with his family. Which was a very, very bad move, because they weren't going to be hers. This whole set-up was just temporary, and she'd better not forget it.

'Thanks, but I need to catch up on some work.' Today was definitely going to be a lab day. A day where she had to fill her mind with chemical formulae and keep all the emotional stuff well at bay.

'But you'll have dinner with us tonight? I'll cook,' he offered.

There was no way she could refuse: Adam's parents would

expect to see something of her. And even though she worked odd hours, the excuse wasn't strong enough to last for their entire visit. 'Thanks. I'll bring pudding.'

And it was just like the previous evening: banter between Adam and his family, drawing her into the charmed circle. Adam stealing kisses in the kitchen, which she went along with even though she was pretty sure his parents weren't going to walk in. And by the time they went back down to her flat, her whole body was tingling.

Your bed's big enough for two, a little voice murmured wickedly in her head.

Yes, but if she offered and he thought she was trying to come on to him, he'd run a mile.

Well, you are trying to come on to him, the little voice continued.

And how pathetic did that make her? She backed off. Fast. Mumbled something about needing an early night. And fled into the bathroom before she did something stupid—like ripping her clothes off and begging him to join her in the shower.

Monday and Tuesday followed the same routine, as Adam had taken annual leave to spend time with his parents, and Kerry really did have site meetings booked. But she'd cleared her day for Wednesday, when Adam was back on shift, and took Adam's parents to her lab.

Spending the day with Adam's parents was like the day she would have once wanted to spend with her own, showing them round her lab and explaining about her job and even showing them some footage of major displays she'd done. Though Adam's parents were far more appreciative than hers would ever have been, asking questions and drawing her out.

'You can tell why Adam fell in love with you,' Moira said on the way home. 'You're very different from his usual women.'

'You mean, I'm not tall and glamorous,' Kerry said wryly.

'You're not a fake,' Moira said.

Ha. If only that were the truth. Kerry was definitely a fake. The fiancée who wasn't really a fiancée. Just a friend who was acting. For the very best of reasons—but the more she got to know Adam's family, the guiltier she felt about the deception.

'And you're not an airhead, either. He can talk to you— and anyone can see he's serious about you.'

Seriously *acting,* Kerry thought. He liked her, but that was as far as it went. She hated the way she and Adam were lying to his parents, but what option did they have?

'It's in his eyes,' Moira continued. 'The way he looks at you. And the way you look at him.'

Oh, help, Kerry thought. Adam could act well, but she couldn't. She just hoped that Adam hadn't picked up on the eye business. If he had any idea that she was falling for him, it would be—well, messy, to say the least. And she definitely wouldn't see him again.

'I'm so glad he found you,' Moira said. 'So glad he finally saw what was under his nose all the while.'

'Me, too,' Kerry said, somehow forcing herself to smile.

CHAPTER TEN

WHEN the McRaes went back to Scotland later in the week, Kerry saw them off at the airport with Adam. Afterwards, he dropped her off at her flat. 'I'd better move my stuff back upstairs,' he said.

'Need a hand?' she asked.

'No, it's fine. It won't take me long. Then I'm going to head to the dry ski slopes for a bit. Catch you later.'

'Sure.' Kerry suppressed the disappointment that he didn't want to spend time with her. Well, there was no need, now his parents had gone back to Scotland. The play-acting was over, for the time being.

Strange how her flat felt so empty. After Adam had left, moving her things back into the gaps she'd created for him felt...odd. Almost as if she were putting her life together again after a relationship had crashed and burned. Which was stupid. She and Adam didn't have a relationship. They were just friends.

Though it didn't stop her missing him. Particularly the next morning—she'd got used to him coming into her room before breakfast with a mug of coffee, then sitting on the edge of the bed drinking from his own mug and talking to her about his day and asking her questions about her own plans. She loved just watching him talk—Adam had the most beautiful mouth she'd ever seen.

Crazy how just a few days had made such a big impact on her life.

'Stop dreaming. It's not going to happen,' she told herself crossly. Adam wasn't going to wake up one morning and fall in love with her and want to move in together permanently. A long-term relationship just wasn't in his plans—not with anyone, and certainly not with her. And she'd be very, very stupid if she let herself hope.

'Did you get out the wrong side of bed this morning, or something?' Stacey asked.

'What?' Adam stared at her, frowning. 'What are you talking about?'

'You're biting everyone's heads off,' the charge nurse told him. 'And you've made our student nurse cry. On her first day here, too.'

He grimaced. 'Ah, hell. Sorry. I'll go and apologise.'

'Good. And I hope it's not going to happen again.'

'It won't,' Adam promised. 'I'll explain to her I'm not usually like this.'

'No. They're normally in tears because of you for another reason,' Stacey said wryly. 'Though the grapevine says you've given up dating.'

'Temporarily.'

Stacey's mouth quirked. 'That's probably what's wrong with you, then. Withdrawal symptoms.'

Adam pulled a face at her. 'Thank you for your diagnosis, Charge Nurse Burroughs. But I'm fine. Absolutely peachy.'

Though maybe, he thought, Stacey had a point. He was out of sorts because he wasn't dating. And, if he was honest with himself, it was because he wasn't dating one woman in particular. The woman he'd been living with, for the last week.

And now he was back in his own space. He should be relishing the freedom. Instead, he felt as if something was missing. Something important. Something he needed in his space as much as oxygen.

Ah, hell. He shouldn't be missing Kerry like this. She was his friend. She didn't do relationships, and if he asked her out for real she'd run a mile.

Maybe he should get his little black book out. Find himself someone to have fun with for a while. Except he knew there was no point in bothering: nobody in that book could hold a candle to Kerry Francis.

Which left an important question: what was he going to do about it?

He was no nearer to finding the answer late on Monday morning, when he got a call from his mother in the middle of his shift. 'Adam, I think you should know I've just called an ambulance. I think your father's having another heart attack.'

Adam's stomach dropped. 'I'm on my way.'

'No, love. There's nothing you can do right now.'

'I'm on my way,' he repeated. This was serious and, come hell or high water, he'd get to his father's bedside.

He'd just arranged with his consultant to get a locum in for the rest of his shift and the next few days when there was another call for him.

He grabbed the phone, fearing the worst. 'Mum?'

'No. Me,' Kerry said. 'Your mum's just called me and told me what's going on. I'm on my way to pick you up and drive you to the airport. I've packed you some clothes and what have you.'

Kerry. Sounding cool, calm and—and the one person he

wanted to speak to most in the world, right now. And she'd packed him a bag already? 'You're amazing. Thank you,' he said. 'Have you left already?'

'What, after the lectures you give about the people you've had to patch up in Resus because they were stupid enough to drive and use a mobile phone at the same time?'

Hope flared within him. 'In that case, since you're still at home…would you come with me?'

'To Edinburgh, you mean?' She sounded surprised.

'Yeah. It'd mean a lot to my parents.' It would mean a lot to him, too. Though he didn't know how to tell her that without scaring her away. 'Just for a couple of days. If you're not up to your eyes in work.'

'I am, but I can do most of my stuff remotely if I bring my laptop. OK. If you can get a flight, I'll come with you. Though I'll pay for my own seat. No arguments.'

'No arguments. And thank you,' he said softly.

'I'll meet you at the hospital entrance. I'll be as quick as I can.'

'Don't get a speeding fine.'

She laughed. 'I'm not the one who drives a fast car.'

'You can drive my car if you want to.'

She laughed again. 'And have you panicking the whole time in case I put a teensy little dent in the door when I park it? No, thanks. I'm not insured to drive it, anyway. So I'll stick to mine.' It was small and practical—like Kerry herself.

'I'll be waiting by the entrance,' he promised. 'I'll book our flights now.'

Amazingly, he managed to get them adjacent seats. And while he carried their luggage from the car park, Kerry was on her mobile phone, rearranging the meetings she had set up for the rest of the week.

'Sorted,' she said, switching her phone off as they arrived at the check-in desk.

'Thanks. I really appreciate this, Kerry.'

'No problem. That's what friends are for.'

Yes. But he didn't want her to be just his friend any more. He wanted her to be his lover. The woman in his life. The woman he came home to.

He was silent as they got on the plane and found their seats. People around them were chatting, laughing, but all he could think about was what he might have to face in Scotland. Second heart attacks were often worse than the first. If his dad died...

'Hey.' Kerry's hand covered his and her fingers squeezed his lightly. 'Stop brooding. It might not be as bad as you think.'

'What if it is?'

'Then you'll find the strength to face it. Don't borrow trouble.'

He sighed, and laced his fingers properly through hers. 'Sorry. I shouldn't be leaning on you like this. It's weak.'

'Actually,' she corrected, 'it's strong—because you know you need support and you're man enough to ask for it.'

'Yeah.' He bit his lip. 'I might need to ask you something else.'

'What?'

'If Dad's in a bad way...then I'd want him to die happy.'

She frowned. 'Are you asking what I think you're asking?'

He looked her straight in the eye. 'Would you get married to me in Scotland?'

She'd known this was coming. Their fake engagement had just snowballed: right at the start, Adam hadn't even thought his scheme to get his dad to take it easy would actually work. But it had—to the point where they'd had to make the engagement a real one, with a real ring. His parents really believed she was Adam's fiancée. They'd taken her to their hearts.

And now Adam wanted her to get married to him. So if Donald died, he'd die secure in the knowledge that his son was settled.

Completely the wrong reason for getting married.

But Kerry didn't believe in marriage anyway. Not after what she'd seen of her parents' marriage. And this wasn't going to be a real marriage anyway—was it?

'I know we never intended this to happen,' he said softly. 'I didn't even think we'd end up engaged.'

'You want me to marry you.'

'Just until Dad pulls through. Or, if he—' Adam was clearly too choked to finish the sentence. He sucked in a breath. 'We can get divorced quietly later.'

'Which will hurt your mum—and your dad—terribly.' They'd feel abandoned by the girl they'd started to treat as their daughter. And Kerry knew all about that feeling. Not being wanted. Cast aside. She shook her head. 'We can't do that to them. How can you even think about it?'

Adam raked his free hand through his hair. 'I'm sorry. I'm making a mess of this—I'm not thinking straight right now.'

Because he was worried about Donald. She understood that.

'But if we don't get divorced, that means staying married.' He dragged in a breath. 'I never planned to get married. I didn't get the impression you did, either. So perhaps it wouldn't really matter if we stayed married.'

Married to Adam. For now, for always. 'What if one of us needs to get divorced in the future?' she asked.

'You mean, if you met someone?'

Unlikely. It was far more possible that Adam would fall in love with someone. Not that she wanted to voice it. 'Something like that.'

'Then I'd set you free. Of course I would. I wouldn't stand in your way, Kerry.'

Just as he'd expect her to set him free. She was setting herself up for heartache, she knew. But no way could she hurt his parents. Especially now, when Donald was so ill. And maybe, just maybe, she could have Adam for one night.

Their wedding night.

She took a deep breath. 'All right. I'll marry you.'

He drew her hand up to his mouth. Kissed each finger in turn. 'I don't know how to thank you.'

'No need.' He was giving her something—the chance to belong to a family, just for a little while. The chance to belong with *him,* just for a little while.

'Scots law isn't the same as English law,' he said. 'We'll have to fill in forms, and I have a feeling we're supposed to give some ridiculous amount of notice.' His voice roughened. 'We might not even have the time they ask for. Dad's certainly not well enough to travel to London, or even just over the English border.'

She rubbed her thumb against his. 'Look, when we've seen your dad, why don't I go and check things out at the register office? I'll explain the situation—that your dad's seriously ill and we want to get married—and see if there's anything they can do in the circumstances.'

'Would you do that?'

'Of course I will.' Clearly Adam wouldn't want to be away from Donald's bedside. And organising was something she was good at. She'd rather do something practical than hang around in a hospital bedroom, feeling a bit like a spare part.

'I've booked us into the hotel nearest the hospital,' Adam said. 'Separate rooms.'

'That's fine.' Hopefully his mother wouldn't query it. Or

he could say that there were only single rooms left at short notice.

Adam was silent for most of the rest of the journey. But Kerry noticed that he held her hand all the way.

When they finally got to the hospital, Donald was wired up to all kinds of monitors. He looked absolutely terrible— pale and drained. Moira didn't look much better. Adam hugged his mother, then checked his father's notes. 'I'm going to find a consultant,' he said.

'Is something wrong?' Moira asked.

Adam shook his head. 'I'll just be happier when I've talked medicalese to someone. I won't be long. Dad, just try to relax and rest, will you?'

'You, too,' Kerry said to Moira. 'Can I get you a drink or anything?'

'I'd love a whisky,' Donald said.

'You'll stick to water,' Adam said, giving his father a speaking look as he left the room.

'I'll get you a coffee, Moira,' Kerry said. 'And when was the last time you had anything to eat?'

'Don't know. I couldn't,' Moira said, pulling a face.

'You need to keep your strength up. I'll be two minutes, tops,' Kerry said, and went to hunt down a coffee machine. She added sugar, even though she knew Moira didn't take it— hot, sweet drinks were meant to be good for shock—and chose a selection of chocolate bars from the vending machine. 'This is just to keep you going,' she said to Moira.

Adam came back a few minutes later. 'OK. The consultant's hopeful that you're going to be OK, Dad. But you're going to be in here for a good ten days because they need to keep a close eye on you.' He looked at his mother. 'Kerry and I are booked into the hotel across the road. Do you want me to book a room there for you, too, Mum?'

Moira shook her head. 'I'm staying here. Donald and I haven't spent a night apart since our marriage, and we're too old to do something different now.'

'Have you got a change of clothes with you or anything?' Kerry asked.

Moira smiled wryly. 'No, but I can live with that.'

'I can get you some toiletries and underwear, at the very least,' Kerry said.

'Nothing too racy, mind,' Donald said, attempting a smile. 'I'm supposed to be resting.'

'Ah, away with you,' Moira said, but Kerry noticed that the older woman's knuckles were white and she was blinking back tears.

'Everything's going to be fine,' she said softly, hugging Moira. 'Adam and I are here for as long as you need us. We're not going anywhere. In fact, we were talking on the plane.' She glanced at him and gave him the tiniest nod.

'We're going to bring the wedding forward,' Adam said. 'We're going to get married here. Just as soon as we can arrange it.'

'Married? Here?' Moira echoed, looking shocked. 'But…what about your plans?'

'Doesn't matter,' Adam said. 'The most important people at my wedding are my bride, my mum and my dad. Everything else…' He shrugged.

'Everything else is just trappings,' Kerry said softly. 'People are important, not things. And seeing Donald so ill…it's just focused us on what's important.'

'I…' A tear rolled down Moira's cheek. 'What about all your friends, the people you wanted there?'

Kerry gently wiped away the tear with her thumb, and hugged Moira tightly. 'Adam's said it already. The four of us. That's all we need for our wedding.'

'I know they say that when your son gets married, you lose him—but, oh, Kerry, I feel it's not true in this case. I'm gaining a real daughter in you,' Moira said, her voice wobbly. 'And I'm so glad.'

Kerry felt the sting of tears in her own eyes and squeezed them tightly shut. When had she last really felt as if she were a daughter? Marrying Adam would give her the parents she'd always wanted. People who really cared about her. Who wanted her as part of their family.

'It's all going to be OK. Adam and I...we're not going to let you down. Ever,' she added fiercely.

'I'm...I'm just so delighted that you're getting married. And that Donald and I will be there.' Moira sniffed hard. 'I'm not really crying.'

'Women,' Donald said with a cynical air.

But Kerry opened her eyes again, glanced at him and saw that his eyes were suspiciously bright, too.

Moira pulled herself together. 'But—there's such a lot to sort out.'

Kerry nodded. 'We were talking on the plane. I'm going to see the registrar this afternoon, see what needs to be done and when.'

'We'll help with anything you need,' Moira said. 'Well, *I* will. You're staying put,' she said to Donald.

'Thank you,' Kerry said. She glanced at her watch. 'Actually, I'd better go. And I'll get some things on my way back here. Is there anything you need, Donald? Anything that would make you more comfortable?'

'No, lass, I'm fine,' he said. His eyelids looked decidedly droopy. 'I want to celebrate. My only son's getting married to a lovely lass—we couldn't have chosen better for him ourselves. But, oh, I can't keep my eyes open.'

'You need to rest, Dad.' Adam turned to Kerry. 'We'll be in the relatives' room, if you need to get hold of us.'

'I'll switch my mobile on as soon as I'm out of the hospital,' Kerry promised. 'Call me if you need me.'

'Yeah.' He held her close, resting his cheek against her hair.

'It's going to be all right. Really,' she said softly, hugging him back.

Two hours later, Kerry rejoined Adam and Moira in the relatives' room. She handed a couple of carrier bags to Moira. 'Toiletries, underwear and a pile of magazines to keep you going when Donald's asleep and you're at a loose end. And I got Donald some lime juice and some grapes, in case his mouth is dry and he can't face plain boring water.'

'Thank you, love.'

'How did you get on at the registrar's?' Adam asked.

She waved a sheaf of papers at him. 'Good news and bad. You're supposed to fill in the marriage notice four to six weeks before the wedding—the minimum is fifteen days, but our case falls under "exceptional circumstances" so they say we can do it on Friday. We need to give them our birth certificates, too.'

'Which are in London,' Adam said, grimacing.

'We can sort that out.' Kerry wasn't fazed in the slightest. Either she could go back to London and pick up what they needed, or she could ask Trish to send them on. 'I was wondering… Maybe we could marry in the hospital chapel here? Then Adam or I have to collect the schedule of marriage from the registrar in person some time later this week.'

'But organising a wedding in less than a week…' Moira shook her head. 'There's so much to be done.'

Kerry looked thoughtful. 'Not really. It's not going to be a huge wedding so it won't be that complicated. Once the ceremony's organised, I just need a dress and a bouquet, and

Adam needs a suit. We can hire those if need be. Or if I'm going back to London anyway to pick up the documents, I can bring something back with me.'

'Good idea,' Adam said. 'And Mum and I can sort out food while you're in London. The hotel we're staying in is just across the road. If Dad's consultant is happy about it, we can spring Dad out of here for long enough to eat.'

'What if he says that's not a good idea?' Kerry asked.

Adam smiled. 'Then we can talk the hotel into delivering something here and we'll eat in the supremely romantic surroundings known as Dad's room.'

'What about a cake?' Moira said. 'You'll need a wedding cake.'

'One that's big enough to give a piece to all the ward staff,' Adam said. 'So that's it. We can talk to the nearest baker tomorrow. There you go, Mum: wedding organised.'

'It still doesn't feel right to be just the four of us,' Moira said. 'Isn't there someone you'd like to ask, Kerry?'

Kerry shook her head. 'I don't have a family.'

'What about Trish?' Adam asked, surprising her. 'She's your best friend—as good as family.'

'Is Trish the violinist?' Moira asked.

Kerry nodded. 'But she and Adam don't get on.'

'Because she's the scariest woman I've ever met.' Adam shrugged. 'But it's our wedding day, so I'll bury the hatchet if she will.'

'Not in each other,' Kerry warned.

'Make sure you tell *her* that,' Adam said with a grin.

'Yeah. I will.'

'I'll come with you and see the chaplain,' Adam said, sliding his arm round her shoulders and hugging her. 'Have I told you lately that you're the most wonderful woman in the world?'

Her heart missed a beat. He sounded completely sincere. He really did think she was wonderful.

Only because you're helping him and doing something to make his parents happy, her common sense kicked in sourly.

An hour later, it was all agreed. The chaplain would marry them on Friday.

'You're a star,' Adam said softly to Kerry, holding her close. His mouth brushed her earlobe. 'Thank you.'

'No worries.' Unless he kept holding her like this. Because the longer it went on, the more she wanted to untuck his shirt and slide her hands against his bare skin.

She wriggled out of his embrace while she still could. 'Let's go and see your parents. Tell them the news.'

Later that evening, Kerry and Adam headed for their hotel and checked in. As the lift doors closed behind them Adam caught her hand.

'Kerry.'

There was an odd note in his voice. She looked up at him. 'Yes?'

'Look, I know I'm really stretching things here—I booked us separate rooms, but I really don't want to be on my own tonight. Stay with me?'

Her eyes widened. 'Stay with you?'

'I'm not going to leap on you.'

Maybe, but she couldn't promise that she wouldn't leap on *him.*

'Kerry?'

Lord, he looked tired. Bone-deep weary. And she just wanted to make him feel better. If that meant sharing his bed—platonically—then she'd keep herself under control. She took a deep breath. 'All right.'

He didn't let her hand go. Not until he let them into his

room. He offered her first use of the bathroom; she felt slightly self-conscious when she came out, even though she knew her pyjamas weren't exactly revealing. She burrowed under the duvet as soon as she could, and kept the lamp on the bedside table on its lowest setting.

She was going to sleep with Adam tonight.

As in just sleep.

She warned her libido to behave, but even so her mouth went dry when Adam came out of the bathroom, wearing only a pair of boxer shorts. The expression on her face must have given her away, because he smiled. 'I don't usually wear anything in bed. But in the circumstances, I thought you'd be more comfortable if I wore something.'

Oh, Lord. She was so glad she hadn't known that last week. That he'd been sleeping in the room next to hers wearing nothing but her spare duvet and a smile.

'Are you sure you don't want me to go to my own room?' she mumbled.

'Yes.' He climbed into bed beside her. 'I just need you to hold me, Kerry.' He shifted onto his side and rested his head on her shoulder, wrapping his arm round her waist and manoeuvring his legs so that he was curled round her and her legs were draped over his.

'I'm so glad it's you here with me,' he said softly.

For a moment, hope flickered in her heart; then she reminded herself not to be so silly. He wasn't in love with her. He just needed a friend to hold him—and that was precisely what she was doing. One arm round him, holding him close, and the other hand resting along his arm that was wrapped round her waist.

She reached out and switched off the light, then let her hand settle back along his arm again.

'Goodnight,' he murmured.

'Goodnight.' Not that she'd ever be able to fall asleep. This was mad. She'd never spent the night with anyone before. Sex, yes: sleeping, no. She'd never let her lovers that close. Ever.

But Adam was this close. Right here, right now. On the point of falling asleep, admittedly—but all she had to do was turn her head slightly and drop a kiss on his brow. Instigate a proper kiss. Or gently nudge the arm round her waist just a little bit further north.

Or south.

Oh, Lord. She had to do something or she was going to spontaneously combust. Something to concentrate her mind away from Adam.

Combust. Yeah, combustion was good. Incandescence. She mentally went through the list of the chemicals she used most often, and the wavelengths of the light they produced in nanometres.

Halfway through doing the list backwards, she drifted into sleep.

CHAPTER ELEVEN

ON TUESDAY morning, Kerry surfaced slowly, feeling too warm and comfortable to open her eyes.

Then she realised that she was alone in bed.

Where was Adam? She frowned, listening: there was no sound of a shower or the extractor fan going in the bathroom. She rolled over and slid one hand across his side of the bed. Cold. Which meant he'd been gone for a while.

Not his father, surely? Her heart missed a beat. No, of course not. Moira would have called them if anything had happened and Kerry wasn't a particularly heavy sleeper, so the sound of the phone would have woken her. She opened her eyes fully, and saw the note propped against his pillow.

Gone for a swim. A.

So what now? Had he ordered breakfast from room service? Or was he expecting her to meet him in the restaurant downstairs? Typical Adam: acting before he'd thought things through and leaving her to read his mind.

But at least it gave her a breathing space so she wouldn't do anything stupid. If she'd woken up with his body wrapped round hers, this morning, she would've reacted in the obvious way.

Which was not a good idea.

She might be getting married to him later this week, but

it wasn't a real marriage. It was a marriage in name only. And the quicker she got that into her head, the better.

Kerry showered swiftly and dressed. By the time she'd packed her things back in her overnight bag and tidied the room, Adam was back, his hair still wet from his swim and slicked back from his face. Thankfully he was dressed in normal clothes, so he must have showered and dressed in the gym changing rooms.

Then it hit her. She hadn't packed any swimming trunks for him. So had he been swimming *naked*?

The question must have shown on her face, because he looked amused. 'Before you ask, the hotel shop stocks a few essentials for guests. I bought a new pair of swimming trunks.'

'Ah.' She felt the colour rushing to her cheeks. To cover her embarrassment, she asked, 'Have you called the hospital yet?'

'Yes, and Dad had a comfortable night. Ready for breakfast?'

'Sure.'

She admired his detachment. How on earth did he manage it? She was still hot and bothered by the thought of spending the night in his arms. They'd been just sleeping, admittedly, and she'd been wearing pyjamas, but they'd still been wrapped in each other's arms, only a thin piece of material separating their bodies.

Ah, she hated the awkwardness of the morning after. Which was one of the reasons why she never let her lovers stay the night—or stayed with them.

Not that Adam was actually her lover. They'd barely even kissed, let alone touched—and they definitely hadn't touched each other *intimately*.

Oh, Lord. She was quivering just at the idea of it. How sad could she get?

To cover her embarrassment, she went into organisational

mode. 'I'd better ring Trish this morning,' she said. 'And I thought maybe I'd better go back to London later today and get those documents. I'll need to know where you keep your papers.' She paused. 'I'm assuming you haven't been married before.'

'No. Never even been close,' Adam said.

'That makes things easy, then. Me, neither.'

'When are you going to get your dress?'

'Tomorrow morning. Then I'll be back here tomorrow night, and we can sort out the last bits of paperwork on Thursday.'

'And then on Friday afternoon…'

His eyes were unreadable. Did he feel as panicky about this as she did?

'I appreciate this more than I can say, Kerry,' he told her softly.

'No worries.' She needed to get out of this room right now. Before she was tempted to hug him. Kiss him better. And then some. 'Did you say something about breakfast?'

'Yes. I told Mum we'd be over as soon as we'd finished here.'

After breakfast, Kerry packed her things while Adam booked her a flight and a taxi to the airport. And then she called Trish. The phone rang three times, four; just when Kerry expected the answering machine to click in, she heard Trish answer.

'Hi, Trish, it's me. I was hoping you'd be in.'

'And you've given me a welcome break from practising.'

'This early in the day?'

'Rehearsal, really. Lunchtime concert. Have I said lately that I loathe Bruckner?'

Kerry laughed. 'Yes, and you'll play perfectly at the concert. You always do.' She paused. 'Um, Trish, are you busy tomorrow?'

'Don't think so but, hang on, let me check my diary.'

Kerry heard the rustle of pages being turned. 'Nothing I can't move. Why?'

'I need to go shopping.'

Trish chuckled. 'Then I'm your woman! We could go after my concert today, if you like. I can get you a ticket if you're free.'

'Problem. I'm still in Edinburgh.'

'Edinburgh?' Trish echoed, sounding surprised. 'Since when?'

'Last night. Adam's dad had another heart attack. We're going to the hospital in a minute.'

'We? You and Adam?'

'Yes. He's sorting out my flight.'

'So you're going to be back in London tomorrow,' Trish said thoughtfully.

'Later today,' Kerry explained.

'Then come over for dinner,' Trish said. 'Because this sounds to me as if you need to talk.'

'I… Yeah.' This was definitely something Kerry would rather tell her best friend face to face. The phone just wasn't good enough.

'Right. Ring me before you leave your place, and I'll put lasagne in the oven.'

Comfort food. Which Kerry rather thought she'd need.

Donald's colour was better when they reached the ward, and Adam made a beeline for the notes at the foot of the bed. 'Good,' he said, when he'd studied them for a moment. 'How are you feeling, Dad?'

'I'm fine.'

'But you are staying put. No arguments.' Adam kissed his mother. 'How are *you* doing, Mum?'

'I'm all right, love.'

'Hmm. Well, Kerry's going back to London to sort out the documents today. I'll stay with Dad tonight, and you're going to have my room at the hotel.' When Moira was clearly about to protest, he added, 'You need some rest too, Mum. Otherwise how are you going to cope when Dad's allowed home again? I can probably get some compassionate leave to help you out for a bit but, much as I love you both, I have responsibilities in London, too. I can't commute from Inveraillie to London.'

Moira sighed. 'I know, love.'

'I could take some time off, too,' Kerry said.

'But it's coming up to peak firework season. Bonfire Night and New Year. You can't do everything from your computer,' Adam said. 'You have site visits. Not to mention your lab work.'

Kerry shrugged. 'We'll sort something out. But he's right, Moira. You need to rest, too.'

The morning seemed to race by, and then it was time for Kerry to take her taxi to the airport. Adam walked down to the main entrance of the hospital with her.

'Safe journey. Text me when you get home,' he said.

'Will do.'

She was about to climb into the taxi when he said her name. She turned to face him, and he pulled her into his arms. Lowered his head to hers. Brushed his mouth against hers once, twice—and then, when her lips parted, deepened the kiss.

Time stopped. All Kerry was aware of was the warm sweetness of his mouth against hers, the slow exploration of his tongue, the sheer promise of the kiss. This was only the beginning. When they were alone, it would be so very, very much more…

And then the hand at the nape of her neck moved to cup her face instead, and he broke the kiss. 'Later,' he said softly. 'Call me later.'

* * *

All the way on the plane, Kerry replayed the feel of Adam's mouth moving against hers. And by the time she got to London, she was completely confused. She and Adam were just friends. Their engagement wasn't for real. But the way he'd kissed her outside the taxi…it had been the kiss of a lover.

And this was the man she was going to marry on Friday afternoon.

No wonder her head was spinning.

She went back to her flat, unpacked, and took her birth certificate from its file. Adam's was harder to find because he'd just shoved everything in a box and all his papers were mixed in together. Eventually she retrieved it, and put it in an envelope with hers ready to give to the registrar. When she called Trish, the answering machine was on. 'Hi, it's Kerry. On my way.' Then she caught the tube over to Trish and Pete's Victorian terrace in east London.

Pete opened the door and gave her a hug. 'Hi, Kerry. How are you doing?'

'In a bit of a whirl,' she admitted. 'How was the concert at lunchtime?'

'Fine. She played brilliantly, as always.'

'So did you,' Trish said, walking into the hallway and sliding her arms round her husband's waist. 'Right. Time for a girly talk. If you want to escape to the pub, Pete, we'll save you some lasagne.'

'That,' Pete said, 'sounds like a very good idea. Catch you later, Kerry.' He smiled at her, grabbed his jacket from the bentwood stand in the hall and left.

Kerry handed Trish a bottle of wine and a box of chocolates.

'Ah. That looks serious. Come and sit down.' Trish shepherded Kerry into the kitchen and gestured to the kitchen table. She retrieved two glasses and a corkscrew, dealt with the bottle, and poured them both a large glass of wine. 'Right. To friends.'

'To friends,' Kerry echoed.

'So what's going on?'

'I told you this morning—Adam's dad had another heart attack.' Kerry twirled the stem of her glass in her fingers.

'Is he OK?'

'We hope he's going to make a full recovery. But I'm not so sure, because Adam's panicking. And he's a doctor—so he might know something he's not telling the rest of us.'

Trish frowned. 'I really, really hope you're not going to say what I'm afraid you're going to say.'

'What's that?'

'That you're going to get married to Adam. I mean, I've gone along with this fake engagement thing, even though I think it's a bad idea—but marriage?'

'Actually, that's why I'm going shopping,' Kerry said. 'And I need you to help me find a wedding dress.'

'Run that by me again,' Trish said, staring at her through narrowed eyes.

'I need you to help me find a wedding dress.'

'That's what I thought you said. Oh, Kerry, you can't possibly go through with this,' Trish said. 'You don't love each other, so it's all going to end in tears.'

Kerry took a deep breath. Now for the hard bit. 'Trish, I was rather hoping you and Pete would be there. You're the nearest I have to family.' She paused. 'Actually, Adam was the one who suggested it.'

Trish's eyes widened in surprise. 'That's a bit sensitive for him, isn't it?'

'He's not as bad as you think he is.'

Trish scoffed. 'He's a serial womaniser. Everything you told me about your dad… well, Adam's just as bad. Worse.'

'No, Adam's got a good heart,' Kerry corrected.

'He's going to break yours,' Trish warned.

Kerry shrugged. 'So that's a no, then. Shame. I wanted you to be my witness.'

Trish growled in frustration. 'Of course I'd want to be at your wedding—you're my best friend, for goodness' sake—but you're marrying Adam McRae!'

'In name only,' Kerry reminded her.

'I know why you're doing it, but it's wrong, Kerry. People are going to get hurt. Particularly you.'

'Supposing,' Kerry asked softly, 'Adam's dad dies? How will either of us ever forgive ourselves for not trying to make his last few days happy?'

'Oh, now that's a low blow.' Trish blew out a breath. 'All right. But you'll have to kick me when they ask about impediments, or I might stand there and say you can't marry Adam because he's in love with himself.'

Kerry laughed, despite herself. 'He does have a good side, you know—remember, he rescued me the day I moved in. And he really cares about his parents. He's thinking of taking unpaid leave to be with them this week, and again when his dad gets out of hospital.'

'Yeah, but he's… You need someone settled, Kerry, not someone who's going to act as if he's eighteen for the rest of his life. Fast cars, fast women, extreme sports… He's a maniac.'

'He has a good side,' Kerry said quietly. 'You just choose not to see it.'

Trish sighed. 'Let's agree to disagree. So, have you set a date?'

'Yes. Friday.'

'Friday the what?'

'This Friday.'

'This Friday?' Trish stared at her in apparent dismay. 'For goodness' sake, Kerry, that gives you no time at all to find a dress and what have you!'

'Trish, Adam's dad is really ill.' Kerry grimaced. 'And there's something else that might be a problem.'

'What?'

'The wedding's in Edinburgh.'

Trish groaned. 'I don't believe this. Why Edinburgh, for pity's sake?'

'Donald's not well enough to travel. The hospital chaplain's agreed to marry us in the hospital chapel. At least then Donald can just be wheeled down from the ward—and if there's a problem he's in the right place.'

'Oh, Kerry.' Trish shook her head sorrowfully. 'You're absolutely crazy, though I understand why you're doing it. I *think*. All right. We'll be there. On three conditions.'

'Conditions?'

'One, you let me do your hair and make-up before the wedding; two, whatever I give you as a wedding present, you keep when you come back to your senses and get divorced from Adam; and three, I want to play the music for your wedding.'

'We don't need a wedding present. As you keep pointing out, it's not a proper wedding—and anyway Adam and I both have separate houses. If we were getting married for real, we wouldn't actually need anything.' Kerry paused. 'Though, if you really do want to buy something, you could get us a camel instead.'

'A camel?' Trish sounded mystified.

'You know—from one of the charity sites that lets you give some practical aid to countries that need it, like a hive of bees or a camel or a bike for midwives or planting some mango trees.'

Trish smiled. 'I like it. That's a really nice idea.' She sniffed the air. 'Right, the garlic bread's done. Give me two seconds. And we haven't finished this conversation,' she warned, 'so don't think you can wriggle out of it.'

'You really want to play the music for my wedding?' Kerry asked as Trish put an enormous dish of lasagne on the table between them.

'Definitely. I love playing at weddings. It's just a matter of choosing which pieces you like—or you could leave it to me.'

'What have you got in mind?'

'We could go traditional. It's just me and Pete rather than the full quartet, so we're looking at a solo violin and cello, or a duet.' Trish pursed her lips, clearly thinking. 'We could play a pared down version of Handel's "Arrival of the Queen of Sheba" when you walk down the aisle, and Pachelbel's "Canon" when you walk back again with Adam. And Pete can play some solo cello stuff while we're signing the register— something like "The Swan" or an arrangement of a Chopin piano prelude. If it's all OK with the chaplain, that is.'

'I'm sure it will be. But I'll check tomorrow.'

'You're going back to Edinburgh tomorrow?' Trish's eyes widened. 'But I thought we were going shopping in the morning?'

'We are. We have three hours.'

'Three hours to find a wedding dress?' Trish shook her head in disbelief. 'That's no time at all! Especially as most bridal shops have an appointment system. So I think the traditional meringue dress might be a problem.' Then she frowned. 'Adam isn't going to wear a kilt, is he?'

Kerry blinked. 'Oh, Lord. I never thought of that. I'd better call him.'

'Not now,' Trish said. 'Because I'll be too tempted to grab the phone and tell him what I think of him.'

'You're not going to have a fight with him on Friday, are you?' Kerry asked, worried.

'No. But only because I don't want to upset you.' Trish concentrated on her lasagne for a while. 'Right. What we need is a dress that will look fabulous for the wedding, but is also something you can wear out—' she held up her left index finger to forestall a protest '—when you come to see the quartet play, because you really can't keep coming to posh dos wearing trousers.'

'Velvet designer trousers,' Kerry reminded her.

'You need a skirt. And stop trying to distract me. I've got a wedding outfit to plan. If we've got three hours, that gives us two shops maximum. And new shoes are out—you'll have to wear your black court shoes. What are you doing about a bouquet?'

'I thought I'd sort that out in Edinburgh tomorrow.'

'Fresh flowers—you don't have time to have a silk bouquet sorted out. Go for a simple sheaf of hand-tied roses,' Trish advised. 'And you'll need a headdress of some sort. A tiara maybe—I'll put your hair up. The Grace Kelly look would suit you.'

'I'm not sure about this,' Kerry said. 'I don't wear dresses.'

'You do on your wedding day. Even if it isn't a real wedding, you're going to wear a dress. Tomorrow, you have to try on everything I tell you to.'

Kerry really didn't like the sound of this. 'Everything?' she asked warily.

'Yes,' Trish said firmly. 'Though I won't make you try on anything I don't think will be right for you.' She smiled. 'By the time we're finished, you're going to look stunning. Adam won't know what's hit him.'

Kerry was more worried that she wouldn't know what had hit *her*. She was used to seeing Adam in casual clothes, outside work. But when she'd picked him up from the hospital yesterday, he'd been wearing a suit. And he'd looked absolutely gorgeous.

And the way he'd kissed her yesterday…

Oh, Lord. Walking down the aisle to him would be a real test.

By the end of the evening, Trish had it all planned out. 'I'll meet you tomorrow at Oxford Circus tube station. Nine o'clock on the dot. And by the time you have to go back to Edinburgh, we'll have your outfit sorted. This might not be a real wedding, but you're going to look every inch a real bride.'

Kerry called Adam when she left Trish's, but his phone was switched off. Then she remembered that he'd offered to spend the night by his father's bedside, so of course he'd have his phone switched off. He might have a break at some point and check for text messages, though.

R u wearing a kilt? If so, what colour?

She didn't know much about tartan at all—only that different clans had different designs. What colour McRae tartan was, she had no idea. But if he was wearing a kilt, she needed to make sure the dress she bought tomorrow didn't clash with it.

She was surfing the net to kill time when her phone rang. She answered it absently.

'Hi. Just got your message.'

Adam. And her whole body thrilled to hear his voice. Bad. Very bad.

'How's your dad?' she asked.

'He's doing OK. So's Mum.'

'Good. So are you wearing a kilt?'

'No. I'm proud of my heritage and all that, but I am not wearing a kilt.'

'Hey. Women are supposed to fall at your feet when you wear a kilt,' she teased.

He laughed. 'That's just an excuse to look up it and see what Scotsmen really wear under them.'

She was glad he couldn't see her right now—her face felt as if it were brick-red. And she was cross with herself for even speculating what Adam might or might not wear under a kilt. 'Kilt and sporran. One to me.'

'Oh, that's unfair. Below the belt,' Adam accused. 'Literally.'

Would her mind *please* stop wandering? What Adam wore below his belt was none of her business.

'Right. Fife and drum. One all,' he said. 'So you're coming back tomorrow?'

'Evening,' she confirmed. 'Which is probably too late to see the registrar. Can you check with the chaplain if it's OK to have a violin and cello playing us down the aisle?'

'So Trish and her husband are definitely coming?'

'Pete,' she reminded him. 'Yes.'

Adam paused. 'I'm glad you'll have someone at the wedding on your side.'

'Why?'

'Because Mum feels she's doing us out of a proper wedding. Actually, there's something I need to tell you.'

The base of Kerry's spine prickled. 'What?'

'She's mobilised the family. Called them and asked them to come on Friday. I had no idea she'd organised it until it was too late.' He coughed. 'I can't exactly uninvite them.'

'Uninvite whom?'

'My aunts and uncles. Some of my cousins.'

She was going to have to do this in front of a whole fleet of McRaes? Oh, no.

He made no comment about her silence. 'The good news is, the consultant's agreed to spring Dad for a couple of hours. I'm going to talk to the hotel tomorrow about a meal.'

He sounded so impersonal, they could have been organising a firework display. Not their wedding. Then again, this wasn't a proper wedding, was it?

'Sounds fine.'

'Kerry? Something else I need to talk to you about. I owe you an apology. I, um, got carried away when I saw you off this morning.'

Decoded: *that kiss was a mistake. It didn't mean anything.* Well, she knew that. 'You're worried about your dad. It's not surprising you're a bit emotional and you're acting a bit out of character.' She took a deep breath, damping down the surge of hurt. 'I'll see you tomorrow. I'll check into the hotel before I come over—assuming that you did sort me a room?'

'I'm sure it's booked,' he promised. 'Night. Sleep well.'

She doubted it, somehow. 'Yeah. You too.'

When she'd replaced the receiver, she switched off the computer and put on a Bach CD. That bloody kiss...she wished it had never happened. Because then she wouldn't have started to hope.

Trish was definitely right about this. It was all going to end in tears. And they'd all be hers.

CHAPTER TWELVE

BY TEN o'clock the next morning, Trish had persuaded Kerry into trying on a strapless dress. A dress made out of red silk georgette.

'It's late autumn. In Scotland. It'll be cold,' Kerry protested. 'I'm going to freeze.'

'No, you're not. It's an indoor wedding. And that dress looks stunning with your colouring. You *have* to have it.' Trish stood with her hands on her hips. 'You have to look fantastic. You can't slouch down the aisle in smart trousers and a shirt. You need a dress. This dress, to be precise.'

Kerry knew when she was beaten.

'Shoes,' Trish demanded next. 'We have to get some. You can't wear black shoes with a dress that colour.'

'Why not?'

Trish rolled her eyes. 'Listen, you made me your wedding style co-ordinator. Which means you do what I say. We now have two hours to get the rest of your outfit. We're going shoe-shopping.'

Kerry didn't do shoes. She had a pair of trainers, three pairs of boots and her medium-heeled black court shoes. Trish had thirty pairs, all kept in their original box and neatly labelled. Way, way out of Kerry's comprehension.

By eleven, Trish had found the perfect shoes to go with the dress, a new set of underwear—'Yes, I know the groom's not actually going to see it, but gorgeous lingerie is the best confidence booster there is, so it's worth every penny'—and a length of material that she informed Kerry just needed hemming and it would be the perfect stole. By twelve, she'd sorted out a tiara and veil, and written strict instructions for Kerry to give to the florist about buttonholes and the bouquet.

'This,' Trish said, 'is most definitely going to be a day to remember.'

Kerry wasn't quite so sure, but she wasn't about to voice her doubts to her best friend. She knew Trish already had doubts enough for both of them. 'See you Friday, then.' She hugged Trish. 'And thanks for helping me with this today.'

'My pleasure.' Trish hugged her back. 'I'll see you Friday morning in your hotel. I'll bring your stole with me.'

From that moment on, time seemed to vanish. Kerry had already packed the rest of the things she needed for Edinburgh; once she was back in her flat she laid the dress on the top of everything else in her suitcase, so it wouldn't crush, then headed for the airport. And then she was back in Edinburgh, checking into her room and hanging her dress in the wardrobe. She texted Adam to let him know she was back, and headed straight for the register office; she had just enough time to drop off the documents and order her flowers before everywhere closed for the night.

Adam didn't ask her to stay with him that night; she wasn't sure if she was more relieved or disappointed. Thursday was spent sorting out paperwork, and Moira insisted on tradition, so Kerry wasn't to see Adam at all from midnight on Thursday. And then it was Friday morning. She was pacing the room, feeling sick with nerves and wondering why the hell she was putting herself through this, when the reception desk buzzed up to her room.

'Mrs Henderson to see you, madam.'

'Thank you. Please send her up.'

A couple of minutes later, there was a knock on her door. Kerry opened it and hugged Trish. 'I'm so glad you're here.'

'I promised. Are the flowers here yet?'

'No. But they should be here any minute now.'

'Good. Pete's sorting out our room and what have you, but I'm changing here with you.' She waved an overnight bag at Kerry. 'And I'm staying with you until about ten minutes before you walk down the aisle. I'm only going then because otherwise you'll only get half of Pachelbel—and I suppose we'd better get the buttonhole to the groom,' she added grudgingly. 'Now, before we get to the important bit—have you had breakfast?'

'No,' Kerry admitted. 'I'm too nervous.' There weren't any butterflies in her stomach; instead, there was a whole herd of elephants crashing round. 'I know it's not a proper wedding, but…I feel sick,' she muttered.

'Pre-wedding jitters. You need to eat.' Trish grabbed the phone and ordered yoghurt, fruit and porridge from room service.

'Porridge?' Kerry asked, surprised.

'You need something substantial. We won't have time for lunch. So you're having porridge.'

It was absolutely ridiculous, feeling this nervous, Kerry told herself crossly. It wasn't as if she were marrying Adam for real—well, it was *legally* real, but she wasn't the love of Adam's life. It was a wedding in name only.

As if Trish had picked up on Kerry's thoughts, she said, 'I still think it's a bad idea, getting married when you have no intention of keeping those wedding vows. You're not going to love, honour and cherish—' She stopped abruptly and stared at her best friend. 'Oh, hell. You are, aren't you? But he isn't.' She raked a hand through her hair. 'Kerry, it's not too late to back out.'

'Yes, it is. But don't worry about me. I'll be fine.'

'Hmm.' Trish looked less than convinced. 'Does he know how you feel about him?'

'No.' And nothing would ever drag it from her. Adam was too much like her father. Love 'em and leave 'em. And never again would Kerry put herself in a position where she could be abandoned.

Trish squeezed Kerry's hands. 'Are you sure you want to go through with this?'

'Like you said, it's pre-wedding jitters,' Kerry said lightly. 'Honestly. It's all going to be fine.'

Before Trish could argue further, breakfast arrived. Kerry forced herself to eat a bowl of porridge, even though she couldn't taste anything. Then the flowers arrived. And then it was time to get ready. Hair, make-up, nails—and finally her dress.

'Right. Wedding traditions. Something old—it's supposed to be your shoes, but you didn't have any shoes the right colour.' Trish frowned. 'Something old?'

'My watch.'

'Right. Something new: that's your dress. Something borrowed.' She rummaged in her handbag and took out a narrow box. 'These are my lucky pearls. The ones I wear when I'm playing a concert.'

Kerry knew exactly what her best friend was saying. That she needed all the luck in the world, if she was going through with this marriage. 'Thank you,' she said softly.

Trish fastened the choker round Kerry's neck. 'Perfect.

Something blue…oh, I sorted that, too.' She handed Kerry a small carrier bag.

Kerry took a peek and burst out laughing. 'A garter.'

'It's traditional. Though, as Pete's going to take most of the photographs, he won't make you hitch your dress up to show everyone.'

'I'm glad to hear it. Especially as this will be the first time I've met most of Adam's family.'

'I thought you said it was just his parents?'

'His mum felt they were doing us out of a proper wedding. I'm not actually sure how many people are going to be there,' Kerry admitted. 'But Adam's sorted out the reception.'

'Hmm,' was all Trish said. 'Right. Smile for me,' she added, taking a digital camera from her bag. 'You look fabulous.'

Kerry smiled awkwardly.

'Real smile. Think of your favourite actor. Imagine you're about to walk down the aisle to him.'

She remembered a similar conversation with Adam, when she'd thought how he shared the same attributes as the actor in question: tall, dark, charming and impossibly good-looking. With dimples. And a look in his eyes that made her heart feel as if it were turning somersaults.

She smiled.

'Perfect,' Trish said softly. She glanced at her watch. 'And we're dead on time. I'm going across the road now to sort out buttonholes and my violin. You follow in ten minutes. If you change your mind, just text me, and I'll come back and whisk you off to the airport.'

'I'm not going to change my mind,' Kerry said. Though part of her was saying she was completely, utterly crazy. Marrying a man she loved—but who didn't love her back.

* * *

Adam glanced at his watch. Ten minutes to go. 'Are you OK, Dad?' he asked.

'Yes. It should be me saying that to you,' Donald said wryly. 'Stop fussing.'

'If you feel even the slightest bit unwell, I want you to say,' Adam said. 'Promise me.'

'I'm absolutely fine.' Donald sighed. 'Stop *fussing*.'

'Promise, or I'll cancel the wedding,' Adam warned.

'All right. I promise.'

'Good.' Adam smiled and glanced at his watch again. Nine and a half minutes.

And then the door at the back opened.

He turned automatically—even though he knew it wouldn't be Kerry, because she'd be exactly on time—and took a deep breath as Trish walked in. He'd promised Kerry he wouldn't fight with her best friend today. All right. He'd do this. He'd be nice to the diva. He forced himself to smile at her and lift up a hand in greeting.

She strode down the aisle towards him. 'Buttonholes. As promised.'

Deep red roses. Adam raised an eyebrow. 'Does this match Kerry's bouquet?'

'You'll see soon enough.' Trish gave him a tight smile. 'Hello. You must be Mr and Mrs McRae,' she said to Donald and Moira. 'I'm Trish Henderson, Kerry's best friend stroke chief bridesmaid stroke witness stroke musician—I see you've already met my husband.' She smiled across at Pete, who was tuning her violin for her. 'Sorry I didn't come across to meet you earlier—I was doing Kerry's hair and make-up.'

'Donald and Moira,' Moira said. 'Pleased to meet you. I still can't quite believe this is happening. Organising a wedding in less than a week...' She shook her head in disbelief.

'Ah, but we're talking about Kerry. Best organiser I know,' Trish said. 'And it helps having mobile phones.'

Yeah. Adam had had several text messages from Trish, this week. Most of them abrupt, though they'd all been the right side of civil. Just.

'Pete's doing the photography,' Trish said. 'Just as well, because Kerry loathes having her photo taken.' She glanced at Adam. 'I need to do your buttonhole—come over here and give your parents a little bit of space to sort theirs.'

Adam's gaze narrowed. He didn't like the sound of this.

'I want a word,' she muttered.

His heart dropped. This was beginning to sound scary. 'Has Kerry changed her mind?' he said, keeping his voice too low for his parents to hear.

'No,' Trish said softly, 'but I want you to know that if you hurt her, I'll personally disembowel you. With my violin bow.'

Adam took a deep breath. 'If I hurt her, then you have my full permission to do that,' he said equally softly. 'Whatever you think of me, I care about Kerry. A lot.'

Her face was full of suspicion.

'We're on the same side, Trish. Maybe it's time we stopped fighting. This is my wedding day—mine and Kerry's wedding day.' He swallowed hard. 'I don't want anything to go wrong. I don't want Kerry upset—or my parents. You know the full situation.'

She nodded. 'OK, got you. I don't want anyone upset either. I'll play nice as long as you do.'

'Thank you.'

Trish finished arranging his buttonhole, and took her position next to Pete with the violin.

Adam didn't dare look at his watch.

Would Kerry be late?

The buzz of quiet conversation began to spread through the chapel. His family was clearly wondering just what sort of woman had finally caught his heart. He knew he had a reputation for dating beautiful women. How would they react to seeing the girl next door? Would they see through the charade straight away, realise that this wasn't a real marriage? Or would they realise that he'd actually done what he'd claimed, and fallen in love with a girl who'd been his friend for a long time?

A girl who was marrying him—and yet not marrying him, at the same time.

Kerry stared at the closed door to the chapel.

It wasn't too late. As Trish had told her, it really wasn't too late. She could turn round right now and just walk away.

But how could she let Adam down? She'd promised.

OK, so she'd broken one of the rules. This was supposed to be a no-strings arrangement, something where they'd walk away afterwards and still be friends. She hadn't been supposed to fall in love with him. But he didn't know that. It wasn't his fault.

So she'd be brave. Walk down the aisle towards him. Promise to love and cherish—and although he'd be convinced she was acting, the words would come straight from her heart.

Quietly, she opened the chapel door and slipped inside. Lord, there were more people than she'd expected. On both sides—clearly Adam or Moira or Trish had directed them to fill up the spaces so it didn't look as if she was a waif and stray. Even though she was one, strictly speaking.

And there was Adam. She could only see the back of him, but it was enough to make her heart beat faster. Broad shoulders, narrow hips, gorgeous backside. If he turned round, he'd give her that smile, the one that made his dimple show and his eyes sparkle and melted her heart.

The man she was going to marry.

The man who liked her—a lot—but didn't love her.

This might well turn out to be her biggest mistake ever.

It was too late to change her mind now. She forced herself to smile—even though people wouldn't really see her face through the veil, she needed to be smiling—and gave Trish the nod.

Adam laced his fingers together. How could time just slide and stretch like this? Seconds felt like hours.

Or supposing he'd been standing there longer than he thought? Supposing she'd lost her nerve and couldn't go through with it? Supposing—

And then he heard the first notes of the 'Arrival of the Queen of Sheba'. There was a collective gasp.

Adam turned round.

Kerry was walking down the aisle towards him. Alone. Brave and…

His jaw dropped.

It was as if he were seeing her for the first time. Well, in some respects it *was* the first time. The first time he'd ever seen her wear a dress. And what a dress. Deep red strapless silk georgette, with a boned bodice and ballerina-length skirt. Matching shoes with kitten heels. She was carrying a sheaf of deep red and gold roses, highlighting her dress and the gold chiffon stole she was wearing. The stole matched the fifties-style bouffant veil covering her face. Her hair was pinned up and there was a gold tiara in it to keep her veil in place.

She looked stunning. Absolutely stunning. He could see curves he'd never realised lay beneath her usual tailored trousers or ancient jeans. The pearl choker just emphasised the smoothness of the skin, and he itched to unclasp it and trace a line of kisses there, instead.

His whole body was telling him to walk down the aisle to meet her, sweep her up into his arms, and carry her off somewhere very, very private. But he had to stand here. Wait for her. Do the traditional thing. You weren't supposed to run off with your own bride.

And then finally she was standing beside him. Traditionally, he wasn't supposed to lift her veil until the end of the ceremony, but he could see her face through the thin material.

'You look amazing,' he said softly. And she did. It looked as if her make-up was understated and just accented her eyes and mouth.

Oh, Lord, her mouth.

Soft and sweet and enticing. He wanted to kiss her. As he'd kissed her goodbye outside her taxi. A kiss full of promise and wanting and need.

A kiss of love.

Except Kerry didn't love him. She cared for him, as a friend—otherwise she wouldn't be going through this in the first place—but she didn't love him. And after what she'd told him about her parents, he knew she'd never let anyone close enough to love her.

Even him.

The wedding was a blur. He was dimly aware of echoing whatever the chaplain told him to say—the usual Scots vows to be a loving, loyal and faithful husband for as long as they both shall live—but for all he knew he could have been saying it in Martian. He just couldn't take his eyes off Kerry. And every nerve in his body was straining with need. He wanted her so much. Needed to touch her, kiss her.

And then finally—finally—the chaplain pronounced them man and wife.

This was the moment he'd been waiting for. The moment he hadn't told Kerry about. The moment when he hoped that everything would just fall into place without the cracks showing. When he could tell her how he felt without actually telling her. Without it all going wrong.

He turned to face her. And spoke in Gaelic. '*Aon bhodhaig, le cheile bhon là seo a-mach, Aon anam aonaicte, gun sgaradh a chaoidh, Cridhe mo chridhesa, bheir mi dhut mo ghaol, Dean mar a thogras tu leis.*'

He knew Kerry wouldn't understand a word of what he'd just said. But his mother had—and she was dabbing at her eyes. As were all his aunts and the older of his female cousins. And his father and uncles all looked suspiciously misty-eyed, as if reliving the moment they'd said those exact words to their own brides.

> *One body together from this day forward.*
> *One soul united never to be parted.*
> *Heart of my heart, I give you my love.*
> *Do with it as you will.*

'You may kiss the bride,' the chaplain said.

And as Pete began to play the first notes of a soft, sweet cello piece Adam lifted Kerry's veil and gently pushed it back over the top of her tiara, cupped her face in his hands, and brushed his mouth against hers.

Lord, she tasted sweet. He was tempted to let his hands slide down her arms, span her waist and pull her closer— much closer—before he kissed her properly. But things were just too, too complicated.

He settled for holding her hand—he knew she'd be comfortable with that—and they signed the register.

'What did you say to her?' Trish asked him quietly as Kerry was signing the document.

'It's a traditional Gaelic blessing. The men in my family always say it on their wedding day,' Adam said. Wild horses wouldn't drag from him what he'd actually said.

'Hmm.' Her eyes narrowed slightly. 'Just remember what we said earlier.'

'You, too,' he responded tartly.

She gave a tiny nod, then stepped forward to sign her name as a witness.

When they'd finished, Trish resumed her seat and began to play music Adam recognised as something Kerry played to help her relax: Pachelbel's 'Canon'. Pared down to a solo violin and cello, it sounded amazing. And then it was time for them to walk down the aisle, side by side: Dr and Mrs Adam McRae.

Mrs Kerry McRae.

He should have been running for Land's End at top speed at the thought of being tied down. Weirdly, he didn't want to. He actually liked the sound of their names together. Kerry and Adam McRae.

Though Kerry was looking nervous.

He needed to do something, and fast. Kissing her stupid would be a bad move. He could only think of one thing to do, and it would either freak her or make her laugh and diffuse her tension. He just hoped it would be the latter. 'Kerry and Adam,' he muttered out of the side of his mouth. 'Point to me.'

'Negative. Adam and Kerry,' she riposted.

'Ah, but I was doing ladies first.'

'Mr and Mrs, so that makes your name first.' she countered. 'Bride and groom. One up to me.'

'Back to evens with a traditional Northern folk song: the oak and the ash.'

'Carol: the holly and the ivy. Still one up to me.'

He grinned, freed his hand from hers and slid it round her shoulders. 'I have plenty of time to think of another one. The day is young. Ah, yes—night and day.'

She laughed and leaned against him. 'No way. Day and night.' She paused. 'So what did you say to me at the end?'

'A traditional Gaelic blessing,' he said. 'Nothing heavy.' Only that he'd given her his heart. Something he'd never, ever said before. Something he'd never done before.

And he'd meant every single word.

'It sounded beautiful,' she said.

'Yeah.' Like her.

And then they were out of the hospital chapel. Married.

'Hold it right there,' Pete said, materialising in front of them and waving his camera. 'Most of the pictures are going to be at the reception, but you need one here.'

Adam looked at Kerry, and she nodded. 'Sure.'

They posed together with Kerry's bouquet in front of them, and smiled.

'Perfect,' Pete said. 'So where now?'

'Hotel across the road,' Adam said. 'We've had permission to take Dad for a meal.' He smiled at Kerry. 'Tell you something we forgot. Wedding cars.'

She scoffed. 'Considering how close we are to the hotel, it really wouldn't be worth it.'

'Yeah. I suppose you're right.' He looked at his father. 'Though *you* are most definitely not walking,' he warned. 'Kerry and I will push you.'

One of Adam's uncles stepped forward. 'No, you're the

bride and groom. I'll do it.' He laughed. 'Someone ought to take a photo. It's the only time I'll be able to push my big brother around.'

'Watch it, you,' Donald growled, though Kerry was relieved to see he looked amused.

'Thanks, Tom,' Adam said with a smile. 'Kerry, this is my Uncle Tom, otherwise known as the family Lothario.'

'Only because you've gone and made yourself respectable,' his uncle retorted. 'You were winning by miles before today.'

'Ah, but I found myself the perfect woman,' Adam said. 'You're still looking in the wrong places.'

Similar banter ran throughout every conversation Adam had with the other members of his family, and Kerry was convinced she'd never remember everyone's names. Even though everyone was being nice to her, accepting her as part of the McRae family. Part of the clan, even.

And then they were finally in the hotel. Pete took shots of different family groupings, then handed his camera to one of Adam's cousins so he and Trish could pose with the bride and groom.

Although it was a running buffet, tables were still set out, and somehow Adam had organised a seating plan. Not quite a traditional plan—Pete and Trish were in the places where Kerry's parents should have been—but Kerry had just started to relax when someone yelled, 'Speech!'

'Haven't prepared one. Hard luck,' Adam said with a smile and a shrug.

'It's a wedding. We have to have a speech. And as you neglected to have a best man, you can't get out of it,' Tom informed him.

Adam sighed, and stood up. 'I haven't actually prepared a speech because, as you know, we brought the wedding forward a bit. So you'll have to bear with me. Traditionally, the groom's supposed to say how he met the bride. We had an unconventional start, because I broke into her flat. In my defence, she was the girl downstairs—and she'd just locked herself out. Nowadays, I use her spare key rather than a credit card to open her door.' He looked down at her and smiled. 'It took me a while to realise, but Kerry's the only woman I could have married.'

If only they knew, Kerry thought. They all thought he meant she was the love of his life, but she knew the truth: she was the only one who would agree to marry him without strings, for Donald and Moira's sake.

'The best speeches are short and sweet, so I'm going to shut up now. But, before I do, I give you a toast,' Adam said. 'To my beautiful bride.'

'The beautiful bride,' everyone echoed.

Adam sat down. 'OK?' he asked softly.

Kerry nodded. 'OK.'

'We're going to break with tradition again,' Moira said, standing up. 'Adam's kept Kerry very much to himself—he only let us meet her a few weeks ago—but it only took me seconds to feel as if I'd known her for years. She's the kind of girl I dreamed my only son would find. And I can't believe how lucky we are. I'd like you all to raise your glasses and welcome Kerry to our family.'

'Welcome to our family,' everyone said, raising their glasses and then drinking deeply.

'And I'll break with tradition, too,' Trish said, standing up. 'We don't have a best man, but we do have a chief bridesmaid. Kerry's been my best friend since we met at university, and I'm probably the nearest she has to family.'

Kerry exchanged a glance with Adam; he looked as worried as she felt. Surely Trish wouldn't say something *now*?

'So I'd like to welcome Adam to our side,' Trish said. 'I'm reliably informed that his taste in brides is much better than his taste in music, but between us Kerry, Donald and I plan to educate him.'

Adam groaned. 'Someone save me.'

Trish laughed. 'Too late! Ladies and gentlemen, it's my pleasure to give you the bride and groom—and to wish them a long and happy life.'

Not 'together', Kerry noted. Then again, they wouldn't be, so there was no point in wishing all this were real.

'The bride and groom.' Trish's toast echoed through the room.

And then it was time to cut the cake. More photographs. And then a pager bleeped in Adam's pocket.

'They're not calling you back to London on your wedding night, surely?' Tom teased.

Adam laughed. 'I think they have a few people a bit nearer. No, I borrowed a pager from one of the registrars in the heart unit. This is my call to get Dad back over the road.'

'And you didn't even let me toast you properly with a dram,' Donald said in disgust.

'Your consultant would flay me,' Adam said. 'Come on. I'll take you over.'

'I'll do it,' Tom said. 'Give me that pager and I'll return it with your dad.'

'Yes, because Donald and I need to give you your wedding present,' Moira said. She handed Kerry an envelope. 'It's the key to the honeymoon suite. And I've had your things moved there while we were in the chapel.'

'That's… I don't know what to say,' Kerry said.

Moira smiled. 'I know you and Adam said no presents, but you're my daughter now so I have a right to spoil you. And

I want you both to be happy, and start your marriage off the right way. Together. In style.'

Kerry blinked back the tears. 'Thank you,' she whispered hugging first Moira and then Donald.

'Now go. The bride and groom are supposed to leave before the guests,' Moira told them.

'Thank you, Mum,' Adam said, hugging her. 'We'll be over in the morning. But you know where we are if you need us.'

'We won't. Not tonight,' Moira said.

Kerry and Adam said their goodbyes.

And then they were alone, in the lift, on their way up to the honeymoon suite.

CHAPTER THIRTEEN

ADAM looked at Kerry and winced. 'I had no idea they were planning to give us the honeymoon suite. I'm sorry.'

'Not a problem,' she said with a shrug.

'No. These suites are big enough. I can sleep on the couch.'

Maybe the champagne she'd sipped had gone to her head, or maybe she was deluding herself and hearing what she wanted to hear—but she was sure there was something odd in his voice. Something wistful.

Something prompted her to say, 'Adam, it's the only time either of us plans to get married.'

He stared at her. 'Meaning?'

Make or break time. 'What the hell. Let's have a proper wedding night.'

'Are you suggesting...?'

The look in his eyes was so hot that it made her mouth go dry. All she could do was nod.

His eyes turned a very, very intense blue. And as the lift doors opened he lifted her up and carried her out into the corridor.

Kerry couldn't quite believe this was happening. Adam was carrying her through the hotel, as if he were some Scots

chieftain carrying her off to his stronghold. A prized posses-
sion. His bride.

Well, she *was* his bride, in name.

And it looked as if he was going to make her his bride in deed.

He reached the door to their suite. 'Top pocket. Key.'

She fished the key out, and he stooped so she could fit the
card into the slot.

'Well, now, Mrs McRae,' he said huskily, and carried her
over the threshold.

When he set her on her feet, he let her slide down his body.
Close and personal. Close enough for her to register that he
was turned on. That he wanted her.

And then he switched on the lights.

'Oh, Lord,' Kerry said, and burst out laughing.

Balloons. Half a dozen heart-shaped helium-filled balloons
were tied to the lower rail of the four-poster bed. Confetti was
sprinkled all over the bedcover. And there was a single red
rose lying between the pillows. The same rich, deep red as
the roses in her wedding bouquet, which were standing in a
vase.

'That,' Adam said softly, 'gives me an idea.'

Kerry was near to hyperventilating. She had a feeling that
Adam was going to be an inventive lover. And, despite her
past, he was going to surprise her tonight. Take her to the edge
of pleasure, and fall over it with her.

'Hold that thought,' he whispered.

'What thought?' Oh, please don't let her have said that out
loud.

'Whatever put that look on your face. That confetti's going
to get in the way. And I want to move the balloons.' He came
to stand next to her, and brushed his mouth at the sensitive
spot below her ear. 'But the rose...that can stay. I have plans
for it.'

Every single one of Kerry's nerves quivered. An inventive lover? She might just have underestimated him.

She watched him as he untied the balloons and reattached them to a chair, then swept the confetti neatly off the bed into the wastebin. 'No point in making extra work for the poor chambermaids,' he said.

He returned the bin to its place, then fiddled with the radio next to the bed. 'I didn't think to arrange any music. And I can't dance with you to classical music.'

'Dance with me?' she whispered.

'It's traditional to dance together on your wedding night. Even though we don't have an "our song". And you told my mother we danced together, I kissed you, and you saw fireworks inside your head.' He gave her a look so hot, her temperature felt as if it had just risen ten degrees. 'So let's see if you're right. I'm going to dance with you. And then, I'm going to kiss you.'

Promise and threat blended.

She could hardly breathe.

Music floated into the room. 'I knew the local station wouldn't let me down. It's the slushy hour.' He grimaced. 'It wouldn't be my choice, but it's kind of appropriate.'

Chris de Burgh was singing about his lady in red. She didn't particularly like the song, either. But Adam had a point. She was wearing a red dress. Her wedding dress. And right now she was his lady.

Adam held out one hand to her. 'Dance with me, Kerry McRae?'

They hadn't even discussed *that*. And it was pointless going through the rigmarole of changing her name on all her documents—and then changing it back again. 'I'm keeping my own name,' she said, lifting her chin.

He shrugged. 'Whatever you prefer.' He slid his arms

round her waist. 'But not tonight. Tonight, you're Mrs Kerry McRae. My bride. And I claim the first dance.' One hand moved up to her back, pressing her against him, and the other moved to cup her buttocks.

So what could she do but slide her arms round his neck and sway with him in time to the music?

He dipped his head, so his mouth was grazing the curve between her neck and shoulders. 'You look amazing in that dress.' He tilted his hips against her, just for a second, to prove he wasn't just spinning her a line. He really did find her attractive. 'You looked like a fifties' film star when you walked up the aisle. And I think most of the men in the congregation were considering snatching you up and running off with you before you reached the altar.' Another soft kiss. 'Including me.'

'Flannel.'

'No. You hide yourself in your lab or behind your clipboard. But you, Kerry McRae, are one beautiful woman.' Another brush of his lips, this time against her earlobe. And she could feel the warmth of his breath as he whispered. 'And that's a beautiful dress. But I need…' a trail of tiny butterfly kisses along the curve of her jaw '…to…' a kiss at the corner of her mouth '…take…' her lower lip was between his, now, and her eyelids drifted shut as she opened her mouth.

And then he kissed her.

Properly.

A sweet, exploring kiss that suddenly turned explosive. Desire sparked through her, each nerve-end tingling like a starburst, until her whole body was fizzing. Lit up. In flames.

To think she'd wondered if she'd see stars when Adam kissed her. It was much, much more than that. She'd *become* stars.

Her hands were fisted in his hair, and his were dealing with the fastenings at the back of her dress. Three tiny pearly buttons. The slow hiss of the zip. Coolness fanning her skin as the red dress slipped into a pool on the floor.

Adam stopped kissing her, laid his hands on her shoulders and just looked at her. Colour slashed across his cheekbones as he clearly registered the fact that her lingerie matched her dress. A strapless bra and lacy knickers. Hold-up pale grey stockings. The blue garter.

His hands were actually shaking. And so was his voice as he whispered, 'You look fabulous.'

That heat in his eyes was all for her. He wanted her as badly as she wanted him.

But he was fully dressed and she was in her underwear. 'Too many clothes,' she whispered.

'Uh-huh, and I'm going to take them all off you. Very, very slowly. Unwrap my bride.' His voice was husky with desire, and it made her shiver. Deliciously.

'I meant you.' She could barely get the words out.

He gave her a wicked smile. 'So what are you going to do about it, then?'

He was daring her to undress him?

Clearly he thought she was a Miss Goody Two Shoes.

He was about to find out just how bad she could be.

He looked delectable in that suit, but he was going to look even more delectable out of it.

His jacket was the first to go. Just dropped on the floor, like her dress. Then his tie. And then she took his right hand. Undid the button of his shirtsleeve at the cuff. Pushed the material up just enough so she could touch the tip of her tongue to the pulse point.

His intake of breath was audible. She smiled to herself, knowing she'd hardly started. By the time she'd finished, Adam was going to be in the same sort of state that she was. Hot. And very, very bothered.

She did the same with his other cuff. Held his gaze. Undid the button at his collar. And the next. And the next. And then dipped her head and trailed kisses down his breastbone as she undid the rest of the buttons. Dropped to her knees before him. Untucked his shirt. Traced a circle round his navel with the tip of her tongue.

His hands dropped to her shoulders, and she could feel him shivering as she undid the buckle of his belt. Shivering harder as she undid the button and slowly, slowly eased the zip down. Heard his sharp intake of breath as she slid his suit trousers down, leaned closer, and breathed along the line of his erection.

She knew the very second that his control snapped, because he hauled her to her feet and kissed her. Hard.

'Gosh,' he murmured when he finally broke the kiss. 'You just blew my mind.'

She laughed. 'Good.'

'I think I'm going to enjoy this.' His voice was slurred with passion. 'We both are. That, my sweet, is a promise. And I always keep my promises.'

She ran her hands over the breadth of his shoulders. 'Mmm.'

'Not as "mmm" as this.' He traced the edge of her bra with one fingertip, dipping just underneath, and her nipples tightened. She wanted him to touch. Taste. Drive her crazy.

He smiled, as if he could read her thoughts. 'You're wearing more than I am, now.'

'So what are you going to do about it?' She echoed his earlier challenge.

He paused, as if considering something. 'I need to hang your dress up. Step out of it properly.'

She did so; he stepped out of his trousers, getting rid of his socks at the same time, then scooped up her dress and his suit.

'Is this your way of saying you've changed your mind?' she asked, watching him hang up the clothes very carefully.

He turned to her again. 'No.' He smiled. 'Just making us both wait.' His eyes grew hot. 'Like your starbursts. If the whole lot explodes at once, it's spectacular but over in seconds. Wait for each burst to fan out before the next, and the anticipation deepens. The pleasure...' he moistened his lower lip again, and she felt every cell in her body tingle '...lasts.'

Was he saying that they'd make love all night?

Oh-h-h.

Yes.

He smiled at her. 'Now...where was I?' He scooped her up in his arms and carried her to the four-poster bed. 'Firstly, I want you to know that you took my breath away when you walked down the aisle to me—you looked fantastic. I loved your dress and I loved your hair. But what's under your dress gives me even more of a thrill. What's underneath *that* blows my mind. And I need to see your hair down.' He unpinned it swiftly and spread it over the pillow. He rocked back slightly to look at her, and sucked in a breath. 'Amazing,' he said softly. 'Do you have any idea how much you turn me on, Kerry?'

Yes. Because his soft jersey shorts hid absolutely nothing from her view.

And that was the whole point. This was just sex to him. Good sex. Amazing sex. Spectacular sex, even. But still just sex. Whereas for her...it meant a lot more. A hell of a lot more.

It meant making love.

With the man she loved.

The man who couldn't love her back—and she most definitely didn't want him to know how she felt about him. Didn't want his pity. Didn't want him to back away. So she just gave him the sexiest smile she could muster, and hoped he thought she was playing the same game that he was. That this wasn't serious. It was just for tonight.

'Lay on, Macduff,' she teased.

'Mistress McRae, I don't think either of us will be crying, "Hold, enough,"' he informed her huskily.

She had a feeling *that* might be a promise, too.

He traced his finger along the edge of her bra. Dipped just inside, caressing her skin. 'This is pretty. But it needs to go. Lift up.' It took him nanoseconds to release the catch of her bra, whisk the material away and drop it over the edge of the bed.

He stared at her and moistened his lower lip. 'I've been imagining this ever since that moment you were lying on the floor beneath me, covered in paint,' he told her, his voice low and sensual. 'I apologise. I underestimated you.' He drew one finger down the valley between her breasts, and flattened his palm against her abdomen. 'You're beautiful, Kerry. Perfect. But you're still wearing too much. I want you naked.'

That was certainly direct. Nothing she could say to that. So she just smiled.

'This,' he said, removing her garter, 'belongs to me now.' He gave her a lazy, oh, so sexy smile. 'Tradition.'

Then he was smoothing one stocking away. Kerry tipped her head back against the pillows, dragging in a breath as he finally removed it then lifted her foot and kissed the hollow of her ankle. His mouth drifted upwards slowly, teasing her, pausing at a spot behind her knee she'd never even realised was an erogenous zone, then moving up, up, over her thigh. Warm, soft breath against her skin. Tiny nibbling kisses.

She felt herself grow wetter and her thighs parted before she registered what she was doing. But she wanted him to touch her. *Needed* him to touch her.

Right now.

Before she went crazy.

Echoing the way she'd tormented him earlier, he breathed over the silky material covering her sex. Hard enough so she could feel the heat of his mouth. Enough to make her want much, much closer contact.

But before she could slide her fingers into his hair and pull him closer, he'd moved and was kissing his way down her other thigh, rolling her stocking down as he did so.

She could have howled with frustration.

'Patience,' he said solemnly, 'is a virtue.'

'I'm not virtuous!' The words were ripped from her.

'So are you telling me I married…' a nibble at the back of her knee '…a …' his mouth skimmed along her calf '…bad…' his tongue dipped into the hollow of her ankle '…girl?'

'Yes,' she said, shifting up to a sitting position as he finally removed her other stocking.

His eyes glittered with amusement. 'Good. Except you've just made it harder to do what I was intending to do next.' Gently, he pushed her back onto the bed and hooked his thumbs in either side of her knickers.

'Now?' he asked.

If he didn't do it now, she'd go completely insane. She'd never wanted a man as much as she wanted Adam. Ever. 'Now,' she breathed, and lifted her hips.

Keeping his gaze locked with hers so she knew he was doing it on purpose, he slowly, slowly drew the red lacy material down. Blew her a very, very sultry kiss. And looked.

'Oh, yes,' he said huskily, his eyes skimming her body. 'Exquisite. Why the hell did we wait this long?'

She had no idea, either. But he was still wearing his underpants. And she really couldn't wait any longer. 'What's sauce for the goose,' she said, sitting up again and hooking her thumbs in the waistband of his soft jersey shorts.

His eyes glittered. 'Definitely,' he whispered.

Her mouth went dry as she eased the garment down over his hips. Saw just how much he wanted her. 'Adam.' His name came out as a choked gasp.

'I know. Me, too,' he said softly, and helped her remove his shorts completely.

Then he gently pressed her back against the pillows, knelt on the bed beside her and picked up the rose. '"O my Luve's like a red red rose,"' he quoted, his Scots accent much more pronounced than usual. He mirrored the journey of his fingertip earlier, drawing it down the valley between her breasts. 'Soft and sweet, like your skin.' He teased her nipples with it, brushing just the tip of the rose against the hardened peaks until her back was arching; the friction wasn't enough and she wanted more, more, more. 'Dark, like your nipples.'

She shuddered and arched her back as he traced a line with the rose down over her abdomen. Where was he planning to...?

She soon found out. He slid one hand along her thighs, encouraging her to part her legs, and drew the rose along her sex. 'Wet with dew,' he whispered, bringing the rose up into her line of sight again, so she could see her own dampness staining the rose petals.

And then he brushed the rose against his lower lip. Followed the sweep with his tongue. 'Sweet as honey.'

Oh, Lord. Why had she challenged him? He was definitely more of a player than she was. Inventive didn't even begin to cover it.

And then she stopped thinking as he tossed the rose to one side. Leaned over her. Took one nipple into his mouth, scraped his teeth against it lightly but just hard enough to make her gasp and thrust her upper body towards him, and then sucked.

She quivered as he did the same to her other nipple, then blew gently on them in turn.

If he didn't touch her more intimately—and preferably in the next quarter of a second—she was going to go crazy.

But Adam seemed in no hurry. He just worked his way slowly downwards, exploring every centimetre of skin. He stopped to tease her by circling her navel with the tip of his tongue, as she'd done to him when she'd removed his shirt. Payback time. She wriggled impatiently, desperate for him to ease the ache between her thighs. He moved lower, lower, until her hands were fisted in his hair and she was begging him incoherently to use his mouth, take her to the edge.

He stopped.

Breathed.

Teased.

'Adam, I…' She barely recognised her own voice. But she was begging. Definitely begging. 'Please. I need…'

'Release,' he whispered, and settled his mouth on her sweet spot. Just where she needed it most.

Kerry couldn't remember when she'd come so hard or so fast.

When she'd stopped shaking, he moved up to kiss her. 'I haven't finished yet. Not by a long, long way.' He dropped a kiss on the tip of her nose, then walked over to where his suit was hanging up.

God, he was beautiful, Kerry thought. A perfect body, moving with perfect grace.

A perfect *aroused* body, she amended as Adam turned round and walked back to the bed. He took a condom from his wallet and dropped the wallet onto the bedside cabinet. He sat beside her on the four-poster and started to put on the condom.

'My job, I think,' she said softly, shifting and nudging his hand away.

She stroked the cool latex along his shaft, and he shivered. 'Kerry, my self-control's about to go,' he warned.

'Good. Now you know how I just felt. You drove me crazy.'

'Just looking at you does it for me,' he told her, his voice deep with sincerity.

'In that case...' She pushed him back against the pillows, then moved to straddle him. Lowered herself onto him. And as their bodies joined for the first time she felt as if she'd finally found the missing piece of her life.

With Adam, she felt complete.

He tipped his head back against the pillows and exhaled sharply. 'Ah, Kerry, do you have any idea how you make me feel?'

'The same way you make me feel,' she said shakily. 'I really wasn't expecting this.'

His blue, blue gaze caught hers. 'I guessed we'd be good together. I just didn't realise *how* good.' He reached up to cup her breasts, rubbed the pads of his thumbs against her nipples. 'The way you respond to me. The way I respond to you. It's perfect.' He sat up, then, and dipped his head; as he drew one nipple into his mouth she tipped her head back and thrust her hands into his hair, urging him on.

How could he have brought her to the edge again so soon? She could feel her arousal rising, rising, the warmth starting at the soles of her feet and bubbling through her veins, the pressure increasing and finally—

'Kerry,' he gasped, lifting his head and grasping her shoulders.

She clung to him for support, her gaze locked with his, and watched his eyes go glassy as he hit his climax, half a second before her own rocked through her.

Time seemed to stop, and she had no idea how long it was until he rested his cheek against hers and held her close.

'The winter nights are dark in Scotland and very, very long. Which is just as well,' he said softly, 'because I have plans for us for the rest of the night and I need a long, long time.'

She knew it wasn't a boast. It was a promise. And one she'd glory in letting him fulfil.

CHAPTER FOURTEEN

THE next morning, Adam woke, feeling more content than he could ever remember. In a warm, soft bed, with a warm, soft body curled beside him.

His wife.

He shifted as gently as he could so he wouldn't wake Kerry, then leaned on one elbow and just watched her while she slept. How lovely she looked in repose. The barrier she usually kept up against the world had vanished, the wariness gone.

He itched to reach out and run a fingertip along her beautiful cupid's-bow mouth. Wake her with a kiss. Crazy. They'd made love for most of the night, and he still hadn't had enough of her. And when they'd exhausted his stock of condoms...

He couldn't help smiling at the memory of what that beautiful mouth had done to him last night. Kerry hadn't been joking about being a reformed bad girl. And he rather liked the bad girl side of her.

He'd definitely seen fireworks in his head when he'd kissed her. And when he'd touched her. And when he'd entered her, he'd felt a deeper, stronger emotion than he'd ever experienced before. Deeper than desire. Stronger than sex.

Love.

Not that he'd dare tell Kerry. It would make her put up a huge brick wall between them in seconds. Now she'd told him about her parents, he could understand why: she didn't want to rely on anyone again and be let down.

Though he would never let her down. Because now he knew that Kerry Francis—McRae—was the woman he wanted to spend his life with. The problem was, he wasn't quite sure how she felt about him. Or how to tell her how he felt, without scaring her into running away from him.

He watched her until she began to stir. She actually smiled before she opened her eyes—but then the smile vanished when she woke fully and realised where she was. Wariness crept back into her eyes. 'Good morning,' she said, clearly striving to sound cool and calm.

'Good morning.' He stroked her cheek. 'Did you sleep well?'

'Yes, thank you.'

The primness of her reply amused him, and he couldn't help smiling. 'Good. Though we didn't exactly have time for much sleep.'

Her face flamed and she pulled the bedcover protectively around herself—right up to her neck. Considering how intimate he'd been with her last night…

'Kerry. Don't be shy with me.' He twined his fingers round hers. 'Though I admit, I rather like seeing my bride blush.' He smiled. 'Especially as it looks as if you blush all over.'

'Adam, we sh—'

He stopped the words with his fingertip. 'Too late for second thoughts,' he said softly. 'Last night happened, and I don't regret a single moment of it. Real life will force its way back in soon enough, but for now I'd like to stay in the little world we made. Just you and me. On our honeymoon.'

* * *

Honeymoon.

Oh, Lord.

She hadn't thought about this. At all.

'Kerry.' He started playing with the ends of her hair. 'What would you like for breakfast?'

'I…don't mind.'

Had she not been lying flat, the smile he gave her would've made her knees weak and she would've had to sit down. Fast.

'You'd be top of my most-wanted list,' he told her softly, 'but, um, I need to do something first.'

'Call the hospital and see how Donald's doing?'

He smiled. 'That, too. But, no, I was thinking more…re-stocking.'

She knew exactly what he meant. They'd run out of condoms last night. And it sounded as if his plan today was to stay in bed with her and continue what they'd started last night. The idea sent a shockwave of desire through her, and she really couldn't help herself. She licked her lips.

Adam shifted down the bed again and pulled her into his arms. 'In Scotland, traditionally, the bride and groom don't leave their bed for a whole week after the wedding.'

'That's not true.' But her body gave a betraying shiver of anticipation. Supposing they could…?

He moulded the curve of her body with the flat of his palms. 'Well, maybe I exaggerated a little.'

'A lot,' she corrected.

'Mmm.' He nuzzled her shoulder. 'But I was thinking, it's a rather nice tradition. We could always start it.'

A week in bed with Adam. Lazy days and nights spent exploring each other, talking, laughing, making love. Oh-h-h.

Her common sense returned in the nick of time. 'We only had the suite for last night. And we have to go back to

London tomorrow. Our flights are booked. We both have work on Monday.'

In London, where they'd be back to leading separate lives. Just as they'd always agreed. How could the idea hurt so much already?

'I'll see if I can book this suite again for tonight.' He brushed his mouth lightly against hers. 'Kerry…humour me?'

'What?'

'Let's pretend we really are on honeymoon. Do touristy things today. Have dinner together.' He pulled back slightly and looked her straight in the eye. 'And tonight I'll carry you over the threshold of our suite again. Carry you to our bed.'

For the sake of her sanity, she should say no.

But neither her heart nor her mouth were listening. 'Yes.'

His gaze grew hot. 'Hold that thought.'

The thought that they'd keep the dream for a bit longer. She'd be Adam's bride, his love, until the moment they boarded the plane back to London.

He climbed out of bed and pulled some clothes on. 'I'm going to order some breakfast.'

'What about room service?' she asked.

His eyes glittered. 'Not all of our breakfast is coming from the kitchen.' He leaned over the bed and kissed her. Thoroughly. Until her head was spinning.

'Stay put,' he said softly, cupping her face briefly, and left the room.

It was a while before he returned, carrying a tray. 'I sweet-talked the kitchen.'

She frowned. 'How do you mean?'

He tipped his head to indicate the clock.

She glanced at the time and felt her face heat. 'It's way too late for breakfast.'

'Uh-huh. I've called my mum, before you ask. And Dad's

doing fine. We have instructions to go and enjoy ourselves, have lunch out.' Amusement quirked his mouth. 'I didn't think you'd appreciate her knowing that you hadn't even got out of bed yet, let alone had breakfast.'

'I never lie in until eleven o'clock. Ever.'

'It's allowed, today. We're on honeymoon.' He set the tray on the bed, stripped swiftly, then balanced the tray on one hand while he climbed back in next to her.

'So, Mrs McRae. Breakfast.' He cut a slice from a peach and fed it to her.

'Adam, I'm perfectly capable of feeding myself,' she protested when she'd eaten it.

'I know.' He stole a kiss. 'But I'm enjoying myself. Humour me.'

When she bit into the next slice of peach he offered her, a tiny rivulet of juice slid down her throat. Adam took it as his cue: he leaned over and licked her skin clean. Kerry arched her back, baring her throat to him, and the rest of breakfast was forgotten as heat flared between them.

'The coffee's stone-cold,' Adam announced when he finally leaned over to pour them both a cup.

'Your fault,' Kerry said.

'Mmm. And I had such plans. I was going to eat breakfast off you—like that nineteenth-century woman who scandalised people at a society party when she served herself as the dessert.'

'Trust you to know about something like that,' Kerry said with a grin. She slid out of bed, and stretched. 'I'm going to have a shower. On my own,' she emphasised.

'Spoilsport,' he grumbled.

'Otherwise we'll never leave this room,' she said.

'And that's a problem?'

'It is if you want to see your dad and do touristy things.'

'I can think of other things to do. *Interesting* things,' he said, leaning back against the pillows and giving her an indolent smile.

'Hmm.'

'Here's the deal. You shower on your own, now—but you shower with me, tonight.'

Oh, my. The pictures *that* conjured up.

'Deal?' he asked softly.

Kerry didn't trust herself to speak. She nodded, and fled to the bathroom.

She wasn't sure if she was more relieved or disappointed when Adam didn't join her. But having separate showers gave them the best chance of actually leaving their suite.

They dropped in to see Donald and Moira, and were given strict instructions to shoo and enjoy themselves. Adam took her round the touristy bits, pointing out the castle and Arthur's Seat—'Did you know Edinburgh has its own volcano? Extinct, but…'

She laughed. '*Real* fireworks, hmm?'

They wandered along the Royal Mile and then Adam took her off the main thoroughfare to Mary King's Close, the warren of underground hidden streets where people lived in the seventeenth century.

'This is seriously spooky,' she whispered.

He slid his arm round her shoulders and held her close. 'I'll protect you from long-leggedy beasties and things that go bump in the middle of the night.'

Hmm. He couldn't protect her heart from himself, though.

'Next time we come to Edinburgh,' Adam said, 'we'll do the ghost walk. It's even spookier than this.'

Next time.

Except there wouldn't be one.

Kerry pushed the thought away. Not today. Today, she

and Adam had each other. And she was going to live for the moment—seize the day and worry about the future when it came.

Adam showed her his favourite bits of the city, from a room with an incredible ceiling painted sky-blue with stars cut out in glass and edged with gold, to the oldest department store in the city, pointing out the spot in the centre where they always stood a Christmas tree that stretched up past the galleried floors almost to the roof.

'Humour me?' Kerry asked as they wandered through the store.

'What?'

'I want to see what you look like in a kilt. McRae tartan.'

'It's red, so it would've clashed with your dress.'

She shrugged. 'Show me anyway.'

'Dress kilts are usually hired or made to order. There won't necessarily be one available,' he warned.

'Any kilt, then.'

He made a noise of distaste. 'Wear another clan's tartan?'

'I get it.' She put her hands on her hips. 'You're scared. In case there's a stampede of women scared out of the shop by your knobbly knees.'

'I do not,' he said in disgust, 'have knobbly knees.'

She knew that. Like every other part of his anatomy, his knees were perfect. 'Prove it,' she challenged.

'Right. You asked for this.'

He made her sit outside the changing rooms for ages. But the result, Kerry thought when he finally emerged clad in a kilt, sporran, dress shirt, short black 'Prince Charlie' jacket, hose and ghillie shoes, was well worth the wait.

'Satisfied, Mrs McRae? And, yes, it is proper McRae tartan, before you ask.'

'Uh-huh. Mel Gibson, eat your heart out,' she said. Then

she beckoned him over, and whispered, 'So tell me—what *do* Scotsmen wear underneath a kilt?'

He laughed. 'We could scandalise the entire department store, here.'

'You're not going to tell me?'

'Better than that.' He nipped her earlobe gently between his lips, and whispered, 'I'll show you. Come with me into the changing rooms.'

'Adam! We can't!' But an illicit thrill crept down her spine.

'We could.' He regarded her lazily. 'Unless you're chicken.'

Oh-h-h. 'I'm chicken.'

'Pity.' He ran the pad of his thumb over her lower lip. 'Then you'll have to wait until tonight. I'm going to change.'

When Adam returned, dressed in his normal clothing, they wandered through the streets for a little longer; then as the evening darkened they headed back to the hospital to see Adam's parents.

'Well, the smiles on your faces are enough to make me feel a lot better,' Donald said. 'Have you enjoyed your day?'

'Very much so. Edinburgh's a lovely city,' Kerry said.

'But you've barely scratched the surface in a day. And you haven't been to Inveraillie yet,' Moira said. 'Next time you can spare a few days, we'd love to see you. Show you round a bit.'

'I'd love that, too,' Kerry said. Though she knew it wasn't going to happen. This weekend was all the time she'd have with Adam.

'I was going to ask you a favour, love,' Moira said. 'I wondered if I could perhaps have a rose from your bouquet, to press in memory of yesterday?'

'Of course,' Kerry said. 'I was going to leave you my bouquet, actually—to brighten Donald's room up. It won't travel well on the plane.'

'That's kind of you, lass,' Donald said. 'But you'll be taking a rose for yourself? And the lucky heather?'

'Lucky heather?' she asked, mystified.

'It's a Scots tradition,' Adam explained. 'The bride always has a sprig of lucky heather tucked into her bouquet somewhere.'

She frowned. 'I didn't see any heather.'

'Trust me, it'll be there.' He stroked her cheek. 'I'll find it for you when we get back to our room. But we're not going to need luck.'

No. Because it wasn't a real marriage. And these two snatched days weren't quite in real time: they were in a bubble that she knew was going to burst as soon as they left Scotland.

That evening, Kerry and Adam had dinner out in a tiny candlelit restaurant, then walked back to the hotel through the city streets with their arms wrapped round each other. Adam carried her over the threshold again and then to their bed, where he made love to her again, taking it sweet and slow. The next morning, they managed to get downstairs to the restaurant for breakfast, and Kerry knew in her heart that this was the beginning of the end. She'd spent two nights in his arms, now, and that was his limit with any relationship. Adam wasn't going to settle down at all, let alone with her. Wishing was just pointless.

They called in to see Donald and Moira, and Kerry gave them the bouquet; she'd kept back the lucky heather Adam had retrieved from the bouquet the previous evening, and a single rose that she'd pressed within a heavy book she'd bought in Edinburgh. And then it was time for their flight.

Back home.

To the real world.

Where they'd no longer be together.

* * *

Kerry was almost silent on the plane. Adam wanted to take her hand, draw it to his lips, ask her what was wrong. But everything about her screamed 'don't touch'. From the moment the wheels of the plane left the runway in Edinburgh she'd withdrawn from him. And her barriers were all firmly back in place by the time they touched down again.

She was silent on the train, too. And in the taxi he'd hailed just outside their tube station.

Ah, hell. The past two nights had been incredible. He'd planned to ask her to spend tonight with him, too. Take it slowly, day by day, until she trusted him enough to make their marriage a real one.

But from her expression he knew she'd turn him down, and asking her would lead to awkwardness between them. If he pushed her too hard, she'd shut him out of her life completely, and he didn't want that. For once in his life, he was going to have to take this slowly. Persuade her to let him close. Learn to trust him.

Which meant he needed to give her a get-out. Something to save her face. And for Kerry he knew that would have to involve her work. 'I know you must have a pile of things to do, being away from your lab for so long. I'm on early tomorrow and I really ought to call my consultant and get up to speed with what's happening,' he said outside their front doors. 'Thanks for all your help this week. I really appreciate it.'

'No problem.'

Her face was unreadable. Was she relieved or disappointed that he wasn't pushing his company onto her? He couldn't tell. 'See you later,' he said, and unlocked his front door.

Kerry unlocked her own door and went into her flat, feeling miserable. Adam clearly didn't want to spend time with her. He'd already got a list of excuses ready—her work, his work, phone calls. And, despite the fact they'd spent the past two nights in each other's arms, making love, he hadn't even kissed her goodnight.

Oh, hell. Why had she had to fall in love with Adam McRae and his family? 'How stupid can you get?' she asked herself with a grimace. But at least she had her work. She could lose herself in that.

She texted Trish to let her know she was back in London, then headed for her computer and worked through a stack of emails. Her mobile phone beeped a couple of times; she ignored it. When her landline rang, she let it go through to the answering machine. Right now, she wasn't in the mood for talking. To anyone.

'Kerry? I know you're there. Pick up,' Trish demanded. 'If you don't, I'll assume emergency chocolate is needed and I'll come over and lean on your doorbell.'

Kerry picked up the phone. 'I'm here.'

'You OK?' Trish asked.

No. She was nursing a broken heart. But she'd get over it. 'I'm fine. Working.'

'Hmm,' Trish said. 'Pete's had the photos developed. They look pretty good. Meet me for lunch tomorrow, and I'll hand them over.'

'Thanks. Let me know how much I owe you.'

'Wedding present. To go with the camel,' Trish said.

'Thanks.'

'My pleasure.'

They arranged to meet in Chinatown, and Kerry went back to her work. Though she had to force herself to concentrate. And she barely slept that night—her bed felt too wide and too cold without Adam beside her.

Ah, hell. She had to get a grip.

She met Trish as planned; when they'd ordered their meal

and Trish had poured them both a cup of jasmine tea, her friend handed over a packet of photographs. Kerry leafed through them. 'They're very good. If he wasn't an ace cellist, he could have made a real career out of this,' she said.

'Thanks. I'll tell him.'

And then Kerry uncovered a photo that really scared her. One where she and Adam were exchanging a glance. And her feelings for him were written all over her face.

She loved him.

If he saw that picture, he'd know. She couldn't risk that. She removed it from the pile and slid it into a pocket in her handbag. 'Adam might want copies of some of these for his parents. Would that be OK?'

'Sure. Just let us know which ones.' Trish looked at her and frowned. 'You look like hell.'

'I'm fine. Just hungry,' Kerry said lightly. Hungry for something she couldn't have.

Adam—and the feeling that she *belonged*.

CHAPTER FIFTEEN

LATER that afternoon, Kerry scrawled a quick note to Adam across the front of an envelope.

Photos from Friday, in case you want to choose some for your parents.

She slid the photos into the envelope and dropped them through his letterbox.

There was no response, and she was cross with herself for hoping. And even crosser with herself when she found the envelope of photographs on her doormat, with a note in Adam's handwriting beneath hers:

Thanks. Have contacted Trish direct so won't put you out.

How stupid she was, to think that seeing the photos might have made Adam call in to see her. She knew his routine: two nights and it was over. She'd spent their wedding night and the following night in his bed.

Two nights.

Which meant it was over.

And she had a nasty feeling that 'over' also included their friendship.

Adam's phone beeped, and he flicked into the message screen.

He suppressed the lurch of disappointment when he realised the message wasn't from Kerry. Of course it wasn't. She wanted her space. And he'd messed it up between them, rushing her into bed. She just assumed he'd be like her father, having a string of girlfriends and not being able to commit. Right now, he knew she wouldn't even consider the idea that maybe he was different. That he wasn't going to drop her out of his life and move on. That he really did want to be there for her.

He stared at the screen. Trish. Kerry's best friend. Who might just be persuaded to tell him how Kerry was. He called up the message.

Photos ready.

On impulse, rather than texting her to find out where and when to collect them and how much he owed her for them, he rang her.

'Trish Henderson,' she answered crisply.

'Hi, it's Adam. Thank you for sorting out the photos. How much do I owe you?'

'Hang on, I'll look up the receipt.'

He heard paper rustling, as if Trish were rummaging through her handbag, and then she came back on the line and told him.

'When's convenient for me to collect them? Or do you want to send them via Kerry?'

'Actually,' Trish said, 'I want a word with you about Kerry. She's working silly hours.'

To avoid him. He'd already gathered that. 'You know

Kerry,' he said lightly. 'Workaholic doesn't even begin to describe her.'

'I told you on your wedding day, if you hurt her…'

'I know,' he said softly. 'And I know what you think of me. But I care about Kerry—I care about her a lot, and I swear I'd never hurt her knowingly.' He wasn't about to tell Trish how he felt about Kerry. Apart from the fact she wouldn't believe him, he wanted to tell Kerry himself. Once he'd worked out how to tell her without making her bolt. 'Now, about these photos?'

They made arrangements to meet, the following afternoon when he'd finished his shift. Adam only realised how much he'd hoped that Kerry would be there, too, when he arrived at the café and Trish was alone.

He handed her the cash for the photos, plus a box of chocolates.

Trish frowned. 'What are these for?'

'To say thanks for sorting out the reprints. My parents will appreciate them.'

'Yes.'

He sighed at the coolness in her voice. He could guess what was bugging her. 'All right. I've screwed things up. Kerry doesn't appear to be talking to me right now.'

'Indeed.' Trish's voice was frosty in the extreme.

'Has she talked to you about it?' he asked.

Trish folded her arms. 'What do you think?'

'I don't know.' He raked his hand through his hair. 'Otherwise I wouldn't be asking you, would I?'

'Maybe you should ask her,' Trish suggested.

Interesting. It meant she *hadn't* discussed it with Trish. 'You know Kerry. She's self-contained in the extreme.' He sighed. 'And I know why that is, too. I'm probably the only person besides you who knows about her family, and I feel bad because I have the parents she deserves and hers...well, nobody deserves people like that.'

Trish looked at him. 'I meant what I said. If you've hurt her...'

Adam gave her a grim smile. 'Want me to nick my thumb and do a blood-brother promise?'

She pulled a face. 'That's you, you're so bloody *extreme.*'

'Just believe I care about Kerry.' More than cared. He loved her. Which was why, for the first time in his life, he had no idea how to handle the situation. 'Look, I know what you think of me. And I'm guessing you know about Kerry's past.'

Trish nodded.

'Then listen to me—and listen well. I'm not her father. I'm not going to behave in the same way.'

'Tell *her* that.'

'Yeah.' He'd waited long enough. Maybe it was time to act.

He caught the tube home; it was too much of a squash for him to be able to look at the photos during the journey, so he waited until he was home again. Kerry's lights were off, so he guessed that she was at the lab. She'd probably be home late, tired and not in the mood for cooking. Maybe...

He opened his front door; a pile of mail lay on the doormat. All junk. But one of them had a plainish envelope—just what he needed. Bright red, too, so she couldn't miss it. He grabbed a pen from his pocket and scribbled a note on it.

Come up for dinner when you get back. A.

He posted the envelope through her door, then headed up to his kitchen and made coffee.

When he leafed through the photographs again, he came across one that made him suck in a breath and swallow hard.

That photograph definitely hadn't been in the set Kerry

had given him. He would've remembered it. They were looking at each other—and it was very, very obvious that he was in love with her. It was written all over his face.

Why had she taken it out of the set she'd shown him?

There was only one reason he could think of. That she could see he was in love with her—and she didn't feel the same way. Their honeymoon in Edinburgh had been...an aberration. She'd felt sorry for him. Helped him out, and it had gone a little too far. And that was why she was keeping her distance now: she didn't want them to make their marriage the real thing.

The problem was, he did.

Soberly, he addressed an envelope to his parents and slid most of the photographs inside—keeping back the one where it was only too obvious how he felt about Kerry, and one of Kerry on her own, smiling. A smile that could break his heart—because he had a feeling he wasn't likely to see it again for a long, long while.

Kerry scooped up her mail. Junk, junk, what looked like a client letter, junk, bank statement, junk—oh, for goodness' sake, why did credit-card companies have to send her the same offer twice? One big red envelope was loud enough to attract her attention; she didn't need two and, if she wanted a credit card, she'd apply for one! She bared her teeth and dropped the junk mail straight into her recycling box. Then she walked over to her desk, put the bank statement on the middle ready for checking her account in the morning—she wasn't in the mood right now—and opened the letter.

Not a client letter, then: it was from a head-hunter. She scanned it swiftly. 'My client was very impressed with your recent displays...film work...functions...free hand...' Hmm. So she'd be working on film sets and designing displays for star-studded studio parties. And she'd have a free hand. Probably a huge budget. And they'd encourage her to develop the ocean-green firework because it'd be amazing PR for them, too.

Dream job.

Then again, dreams had a habit of collapsing in on themselves. Look at what had happened between her and Adam. A fake engagement that had turned into a marriage, two nights of spectacular sex, and a seriously ruined friendship. He hadn't even bothered to contact her since they'd been back from Edinburgh. Just that note underneath her own on the envelope of their wedding photographs. So it was obvious he didn't want to be part of her life, make their marriage real.

The job was tempting. Very tempting. Doing what she liked doing best, with the security of a steady salary instead of a freelancer's worry whether the client would actually pay up or whether the last display would end up as a bad debt. Better still, it was half a world away from Adam.

An escape.

Though she'd never been a coward. She wasn't going to start running now.

She picked up the envelope, intending to take it out to the recycling box—then, on impulse, filed it. You never knew.

She must have seen his note by now, Adam thought. It had been scrawled on a huge red envelope. How much more attention-grabbing could you get?

The fact that she hadn't responded gave him a very clear signal. She wanted him to back off. Give her space. Or maybe she thought that 'dinner' meant 'I want sex'.

Well, he *did* want sex—now he knew what it was like to make love with Kerry, he wanted to break his unspoken rule of 'twice and it's over'. But he wanted more than that. He wanted to be with her. He wanted Kerry's company. He happened to *like* the serious, quiet scientist downstairs. The one who had a quick mind and a heart-melting smile—and a bad-girl twinkle in her eyes that only he had seen. The one who'd made him see fireworks with his eyes closed.

No, he didn't just like her. He loved her. And he wanted her to love him back.

Looked as if he was right out of luck.

It was another week before Adam got to see Kerry again. And that was only because Kerry was going out of the door at the same time that he was coming in from the dry ski slopes.

'Hey. Long time no see,' he said lightly.

'Busy at work,' she said.

'Uh-huh. Me, too.'

'Can't stop. I'm on my way to a client meeting,' she said. 'See you.'

Ah, hell. He hated this awkwardness between them. He missed her. And even though she'd ignored his last invitation to dinner, he couldn't leave it here. 'There's a new Thai place that's just opened round the corner from the hospital. Fancy trying it out?'

'Sorry.' She smiled apologetically. 'Up to my eyes.'

'Takeaway, then. And I'll wash up.'

'No, you're all right.'

It was only too obvious. She really, really didn't want to be with him.

And if he pushed her much harder, he knew she'd close the door on him completely. Although he was tempted just to go for the Neanderthal approach and haul her over his shoulder and carry her up to his flat, he knew it wouldn't work. Bullying her would make her identify him even more with her dad. In Kerry's world-view, men weren't to be trusted. They let her down when she needed them most, hell-bent on their own pleasure and oblivious to what she needed. So he had to find another way—a better way—of showing her that she could trust him. That he was the man for her.

'Guess I'll see you some time.'

'Yeah.'

He could see the subtext. *Not if I can help it.*

'My parents send their love.'

She just smiled tightly and left.

And Adam, instead of going into his flat, locked his door again and headed for the gym, intending to take himself to the limit in the weights room. So the ache in his body would outweigh the ache in his heart.

Life as normal. Except it couldn't be normal again, Kerry thought, because Adam didn't love her. All right, he'd asked her out for dinner—but it had been because he'd thought he ought to, not because he'd really wanted to. In fact, he'd barely bothered to stay in touch. Even their old, easy friendship had gone. Ruined by their honeymoon. Two nights of passion, and then out of his life.

She remembered the personal ad he'd said would never work. Wanted: fake fiancée. Must be able to make my parents think I really love her and she really loves me. Mustn't get the wrong idea about me actually wanting to marry her.

She'd done the first part: she'd made his parents think he loved her. But she'd screwed up the second part: she hadn't just made Donald and Moira think she loved Adam. The photo from their wedding—the one she'd kept back—was proof enough. She really *had* fallen in love with Adam. And with his family, the way they'd accepted her for who she was.

Now it was the third part. Mustn't get the wrong idea about me actually wanting to marry her.

Bit late, there. Because they had actually married. The problem was, they were only staying together to stop his parents being hurt. They weren't really together. And she couldn't bear to watch Adam move on to the next in his string of girlfriends, fall in love with another woman under the mistletoe.

What she needed was a new start.

And she had a letter in a file that could make a very good new start indeed.

Kerry's phone beeped. She ignored it for a good ten minutes before she checked the message.

Adam.

Smoked salmon and cream cheese. Point to me.

Kerry didn't have the heart to reply.

Ten minutes later, her phone rang. She let it run through to her answering machine.

'Kerry, it's Adam. I know you're there. I can hear your music.'

Yeah. Beethoven. Loudly. What she always played when she felt out of sorts. The choral section of the Ninth Symphony usually made her feel better.

'If you don't pick up, I'll come down and lean on your doorbell. The way you really hate it. Lots of little staccato rings.'

Which they both knew would drive her demented.

So he wasn't going to let this go, then.

Sighing, she picked up the phone. 'All right. What do you want?'

'Just that I've missed you.'

Not as much as she'd missed him. And hell, why did his voice have to sound so warm, like a hug, right when she was trying to bury the memory of his arms around her? 'Oh.'

He ignored the coolness in her voice. 'Come up for dinner.'

'I'm working,' she said automatically.

'And when was the last time you ate a proper meal?'

She sighed. 'Stop nagging.' Adam, her friend, had nagged her about nutrition. Adam, her husband and lover, was another matter entirely.

'I worry about you. And I miss you,' he said again.

Maybe, she thought. But not in the right way.

'I asked you to dinner before and you didn't reply.'

'What? When?'

'I scribbled it on the back of some junk mail, a few days back. A big red envelope. You couldn't have missed it.'

Oh, but she had. She remembered the day when there had been two big red envelopes. And she'd put them straight in the recycling box without looking at either of them. She couldn't even check because the recycling company had collected her box. 'I didn't see any note.'

'Whatever. Come and have dinner with me. Tonight.'

She really wasn't sure she could handle having dinner with him. She'd be way too tempted to throw herself at him. To beg him to take her back to bed.

As if he'd guessed her doubts, he added, 'I have very, very posh ice cream in my freezer. Coffee ice cream.'

Damn. She'd forgotten he knew her weaknesses. And there was something they needed to talk about. Probably sooner rather than later. 'All right,' she agreed reluctantly.

'See you here in half an hour?'

'Half an hour,' she echoed.

'If you're not here, I'll come and fetch you,' he warned. 'I still have your spare key.'

Good point. 'I'll be there.' Then she hung up and continued with her work.

She rang his doorbell with ten seconds to spare.

He strode down the stairs to open the door and gave her

a speaking look. 'I was expecting you. You could have used your key.'

She made a noncommittal sound. It wouldn't have felt right, using her key and letting herself in. As if she belonged there—when they both knew she didn't.

Adam ushered her into his living room. For once, he wasn't playing loud rock music. Wasn't playing anything.

Though he'd set the table in his kitchen. Added a candle. He'd made an effort.

'Wine?' he asked, handing her a glass.

'Thanks.'

'My parents loved the photographs.'

'Good.'

'They were wondering if we could go up to Inveraillie for Hogmanay. New Year.'

She shook her head. 'Sorry, no can do.' New Year. A time of new beginnings. Whereas the next year would only be bringing endings.

'Working?' he guessed.

'Sort of.' She set her glass on the table. 'Actually, there's something we need to talk about.'

'What?'

'Our divorce.'

He frowned. 'What divorce?'

'You said we'd stay together unless one of us needed a divorce,' she reminded him.

His face became completely unreadable. 'Does that mean you've met someone?'

Did he think she was that shallow? She shook her head. 'But I'm leaving. And it'll be easier if we put a divorce in motion before I go.'

'Leaving?' he asked, sounding shocked. 'Since when? Where are you going?'

'I, um, have a new job.'

He frowned again. 'I thought you liked working for yourself?'

'I do. But this is a real opportunity. It's with a film company in Los Angeles. They head-hunted me. They want me to head up their pyrotechnics department, train people and design displays for studio parties.'

He frowned. 'And that's what you really want to do?'

No. What she really wanted was to be with Adam. But it wasn't going to happen. So it was time to move on. Rent out her flat, maybe, if she couldn't sell it. And start a new life half a world away. 'Yes,' she said, lifting her chin. 'I'm going out to the States very early in the new year. So you can put the divorce in motion whenever you want. I'll leave a forwarding address for mail.'

She was leaving.

Going to America.

Starting a new life—without him.

No. It was unthinkable, Kerry being so far away. It'd be as if the world had gone two-dimensional. OK, so they'd barely spoken for the past couple of weeks, and she'd been avoiding him—but he'd known she was there. Known there was only a ceiling-stroke-floor between them for half the time. Known that she was near.

And, stupidly, he'd thought they had time to work it out.

But now things were different. She was leaving. There was no time at all.

'Kerry, I…' *I love you and I don't want you to go.*

Telling her would be the quickest way to make her run for that plane.

So he bit the words back. 'You said early in the new year. So that means you could spend New Year's Eve in Inveraillie?'

She looked at him, her green eyes huge. Hell. She looked tired and out of sorts, and all he wanted was to kiss her better. Kiss her until she stopped hurting. Kiss her until they *both* stopped hurting.

'Please,' he said softly. 'It would mean a lot to…' *me*

'…my parents. My family.'

'As…your wife?'

Yes. 'My friend.' *The love of my life.* 'Whatever. Just come to Scotland for Hogmanay. New Year's Eve. Please?'

She was silent for so long, he was convinced she was going to say no.

Then she sighed. 'All right. New Year's Eve.'

'Thank you.' He resisted the urge to punch the air—just.

She was giving him one last evening. A chance to show her how he felt about her. To offer her a choice—here or LA.

When it came down to it, he didn't really care which. Just as long as she was there with him.

CHAPTER SIXTEEN

'I'M GLAD I caught you,' Adam said at the gate, smiling at Kerry. 'I've booked our tickets. We'll travel up early on New Year's Eve, pick up a hire car at Edinburgh and I'll drive us to Inveraillie. And we can come home again New Year's Day.'

'So I'll be home in time to pack for my flight to LA,' Kerry said.

'Uh-huh.' He glanced at his watch. 'I'm on duty. I'd better go. See you later.'

'See you.' She forced a smile to her face and let herself indoors.

This was stupid, longing for Adam. Even more stupid than longing for her parents, a real family, had been. As a child, she hadn't known any better. As an adult, she knew that Adam wasn't capable of commitment.

There had been a very strange look on his face when she'd mentioned her flight to the States. Relief, probably. She'd be out of his hair. And he'd be able to go back to life as normal.

Kerry's mobile phone beeped.

Santa and elves. Point to me.

She rolled her eyes.

Reindeer and sleigh. One-all.

Two seconds later, her phone rang. 'Hi. What are you doing tomorrow?' Adam asked.

Christmas Day? 'Not a lot.' Trish and Pete had invited her to their house, but Kerry wasn't in the mood for spending time with people. Especially with happily married couples and families. In previous years, it hadn't bothered her. This year, it did—because she was married. In name only. To the man she wanted but had to keep away from; she knew he'd let her down the same way her parents had, and the more time she spent with him the harder it would be for her. The more she'd hurt. 'What about you?'

'I'm working. Doing a late shift. Which is only fair, as I'm taking New Year as leave.' He paused. 'Since we're both at a loose end, why don't we spend it together?'

Yes.

She forced the response back. No way was she going to sound that needy. 'You just said you're working.'

'I am. But I could make us a little Scots supper when I get back. Fresh salmon grilled with butter, steamed veg and new potatoes, followed by cranachan.'

'What's cranachan?'

'A traditional Scots pudding. Oatmeal and cream and honey and whisky liqueur and raspberries. You'll love it.'

She frowned. 'No way do you want to cook after you've been on a late.' Before she could stop herself, she found herself offering, 'Why don't I cook us Christmas dinner?'

'Do you really want to eat turkey and all the trimmings at nine p.m.—maybe later, if I end up staying beyond my shift?' Adam asked.

He was offering her a get-out. And she knew it would be sensible to take it. 'Maybe not.'

'Then I'll do us a cold supper for tomorrow evening. Smoked salmon and oatcakes, or cheese and biscuits.' He laughed. 'Which is two points to me.'

'One point disallowed for cheating: it's cheese and crackers.'

'Hmm. Do you have a Christmas tree?' he asked.

'No.' She'd never really bothered. No point, when she was on her own. Christmas trees were for children, and for families.

'You spend Christmas without a tree?' He sounded aghast. 'That settles it. My place, tomorrow night, quarter past nine. I'll call you if I'm running late. It'll only take two minutes to take stuff out of the fridge and put it on a plate, so you're not putting me out. It'd just be nice to spend the evening together.' He laughed. 'And as it's Christmas I'll even be nice and let you choose the music.'

'I'll hold you to that.'

'Quarter past nine,' he reminded her. 'Don't be late.'

On Christmas Day, Adam's parents rang to wish Kerry a happy Christmas. If only, she thought, but she kept up the pretence that all was well, explaining that Adam had to work a late shift. Then she called her friends to thank them for her gifts and to wish them merry Christmas. And then the hours just stretched. For once, she wasn't in the mood for work, and there was only so much time you could spend playing solitaire on the computer. All the films on TV were ones she'd seen before— or ones that were too family-oriented for her liking.

She spent a while picking out the music she wanted to take up to Adam's. And then finally it was quarter past nine.

Just stop it, she warned herself. He's only asking you over because he's bored, because you were friends before you were stupid enough to have that honeymoon with him, and this is a peace-offering. It's his way of trying to get back the old easiness between you.

Except she wasn't sure she wanted that any more.

And what she did want was out of the question.

She leaned on the doorbell, then let herself in with his spare key.

Adam had a proper Christmas tree in his living room, and she could smell the scent of the needles. The decorations were minimalist—just plain white lights, a garland draped across the mantelpiece, cards hanging from a ribbon—but even so there were more than in her flat. She never bothered trimming up, because Christmas wasn't a time of year she liked very much. She'd spent too many of them watching her dad in a foul mood and her mother in tears.

'Hi.' Adam appeared at the kitchen doorway when she reached the top of the stairs.

His smile still made her weak at the knees. She really should know better. 'Had a good shift?' she asked, striving to sound normal.

'Typical Christmas in the emergency department. Kids with bits of toys stuffed up their noses, and patching up people who've been stuck together for too long with too much booze fuelling the family tension.' He grimaced. 'Still, it's over now.'

'I brought you this.' She handed him a bottle of Margaux.

'Very nice. Thank you.' He beckoned her into the kitchen, took a bottle from the fridge and popped the cork expertly, then poured the wine into two glasses and handed one to her. 'Cheers. Happy Christmas.'

'Champagne?' she asked, watching the bubbles fizz.

'You can't drink red wine with smoked salmon. Well, you could,' he amended, 'but this goes a bit better.'

She really wasn't much of a white wine fan. She took a

cautious sip, and blinked in surprise. 'Actually, this is really nice.'

He gave her a speaking look. 'I wouldn't give you cheap fizz with a bad aftertaste.'

No. She couldn't see the label, but she guessed it was probably vintage, or from some really top-notch winery.

'Happy Christmas,' she said, handing him a wrapped package. A present that it had taken her ages to choose and lots of agonising: what did you buy the man you were married to in name only? Did you buy him the sort of present you'd buy your husband? Or did you buy him the kind of present you'd buy for a friend—the kind of present she hadn't known him quite well enough to buy, last Christmas? In the end she'd copped out and put him in the 'very special friend' category.

'Thank you. Can I open it now?'

'If you like.'

He opened it and looked delighted. 'Oh, yes. Very stylish.' A watch by a very trendy designer. 'Thanks.'

She wasn't sure if she was more relieved or disappointed that he didn't hug her, the way he once would have done.

'Happy Christmas to you, too.' In turn, he handed her a small box.

She opened it and blinked in surprise as she saw the pendant. 'The star sapphire.' From the shop where they'd bought her engagement ring.

'I know it caught your eye. Like a little firework caught in a sphere,' he said. 'Move the stone. Just roll it.'

Mystified, she did as he asked. 'The star moves as you move it.'

'Yeah. It's something to do with tiny needles within the stone and the way the light bounces off the single point where the needles cross.'

'It's lovely. Thank you.'

'Here. Let me fasten it for you.'

When his fingers brushed the skin of her neck, she tingled all the way down to her toes. And she really blessed the fact that her back was to him. She couldn't bear it if he guessed how she felt about him. She really couldn't bear to see the pity on his face.

'Thank you,' she said quietly.

'Let's eat. I'm starving,' he said.

So was she. But not for food.

Stop it, she warned herself. 'You asked me to bring some music.' She handed him a couple of CDs.

'Hmm.' He glanced at the track listing. 'Sure about this?'

'It's Christmas music.'

'I *have* Christmas music.'

A compilation of pop songs, no doubt. The kind of thing she hated. She grimaced. 'Trust me. This is more…tasteful.'

He laughed. 'Are you saying I have no taste?'

'Might be,' she teased back.

Were they falling back into their old relationship? Was it possible for them to be friends again?

As long as she could stop herself remembering what it was like to be in his arms—what it felt like to touch him, kiss him, make love with him—then maybe this was going to be fine.

He put the first disc on. 'Sit down. I'll bring the food through,' he said.

They made short work of the smoked salmon and oatcakes, and just as she took her first spoonful of the cranachan the track switched to her favourite carol.

'I like this,' Adam announced, sounding surprised. 'Is this another medieval one?'

'The words are Victorian,' she said, 'though the music's based on an older Breton carol.' She dipped her spoon back into the bowl. 'This is fabulous. Oats, honey, cream and liqueur?'

'Yup. My grandmother's recipe. I toasted the oatmeal this morning.'

'It's really good.'

He smiled. 'Glad you like it.'

It felt odd, sitting in Adam's living room together, the carol playing quietly in the background and the only illumination in the room being the tiny white lights on the tree. Kerry found herself feeling almost wistful. If only this were all for real. A romantic Christmas with her husband, just the two of them in front of the tree.

But it wasn't for real. Adam was only her husband in name. And she was leaving anyway.

She concentrated on her pudding. But the tension must have shown in her face, because Adam took her empty bowl from her and set it on the floor. 'Turn round.'

'What?'

'Turn round. You're tense. You need the knots taken out of your muscles.'

This was how it had all started. The night he'd massaged her shoulders and asked her if she'd be his fake fiancée.

And this was how it would all end.

Fitting, really. Even though the pain of it made her throat close up.

She turned round and closed her eyes. Adam's hands worked over her neck and shoulders, smoothing out the knots.

Last time, she'd found herself wondering what it would be like if he touched her more intimately. Now, she knew what it was like. And she wasn't strong enough to move away from temptation. She couldn't help swaying backwards slightly, willing him silently to touch her.

Adam's hands stilled.

Time slowed to a faint ripple.

And his hands moved, oh, so slowly, down her back. Slid under the edge of her shirt. Flattened against her midriff. Waiting for a sign.

She closed her eyes, tipped her head back and leaned back so her head was resting against his shoulder. And slowly, slowly, his hands moved up to cup her breasts.

'Kerry,' he whispered. 'Tell me to stop.'

She couldn't.

Christmas was meant to be a time for wishes. And right now she wished this to be real. Wished that he'd want her as much as she wanted him. Wished Adam were hers again. For good, not just for goodbye.

His lips brushed against the nape of her neck and his thumbs teased her nipples. 'I love your scent,' he said softly. 'Not the perfume you're wearing. The scent of your skin. It's soft and sweet and...' His mouth moved slowly along the curve of her shoulder. 'And it drives me crazy,' he whispered, his voice husky.

Just as he drove her crazy.

Knowing even as she did so that she was a fool to herself—that this was only prolonging the agony—she twisted round in his arms. Cupped his face. Touched her mouth to his.

It was like a flame to touch-paper.

The next thing she knew, she was lying on Adam's sofa and his body was covering hers. He'd shifted his weight onto his hands and elbows to ease the pressure on her, and in the soft illumination from the Christmas tree lights she could see the sheer desire on his face.

He shifted slightly so he could undo the button at the neck of her shirt. Worked his way downwards, brushing the tips of his fingers against her skin as he revealed it. 'So soft. So sweet. I need...' He brought his mouth down on hers again.

Kerry had no idea when or how they'd moved, but somehow they'd rolled off the sofa. Adam was lying flat on the rug, she was straddling him, and her shirt was…somewhere.

'My turn,' she said, looking him straight in the eye. Her turn to unbutton his shirt, taking it slow and easy, letting her hands drift over his pectoral muscles.

All hers.

For the last time.

Next week, she'd be half a world away.

She pushed the thought to the back of her mind, and concentrated on Adam. On the dark hair sprinkled across his chest that arrowed down into his jeans. She traced the line with her forefinger, and he shivered, arching up and tipping his head back in offering.

She bent down to kiss the pulse beating hard at the base of his neck, then slowly worked her way down over his flat abdomen. The perfect six-pack, from his workouts at the gym. Balanced by even more perfect legs and bottom, from his sessions on the dry ski slopes.

Too beautiful to be true, she thought.

But he was hers for tonight. Here and now.

'Kerry. I need to…need to see you. Need to touch you. Please.' His voice sounded rusty, as if it was an effort to string words together.

Yeah. She knew how that felt. He blew her mind, too.

She let him guide her upright again. His palms were flat against her shoulder blades, moving in slow, easy circles. Every touch increased her temperature a notch further. A tiny movement, and her bra was unclasped. Fell to the floor, unheeded, as her breasts spilled into his hands.

'Oh, yes. So beautiful,' he whispered, and shifted so he could take one nipple into his mouth. Sucked.

She gasped and slid her fingers into his hair, the pressure

of her fingers against his scalp urging him on. 'Yes,' she hissed when his hands moved to the waistband of her trousers. And still he kept the pace slow and easy, his gaze fixed on hers as he lowered the zipper.

Half of her wanted to rush him, make him rip the rest of her clothes off and just slide deep inside her. But the other half wanted to keep it this slow, so she'd remember every moment in the years to come. She knew there wouldn't be anyone else: Adam McRae had ruined her for any other man.

She let him smooth the material down over her hips. Shifted so he could roll her onto her back and slide her trousers down, down over her thighs, over her calves, over her ankles. His fingers were whisper-light against her skin, teasing her, making her push against him.

'More,' she whispered. 'I need more.'

His hand cupped her sex over the lace of her knickers. 'How much more?'

'Oh-h-h.' The word was dragged out of her. 'More.'

He slid his hand back and forth. The friction was good— so good—but it still wasn't enough. She moved her hand over his, guided his fingers underneath the lace.

He sucked in a breath. 'Kerry. You feel…'

Hot. Wet. As if she wanted him just as much as he wanted her.

It took him seconds to get rid of his jeans.

Seconds—oh, way too many seconds—to find his wallet and drag out a condom.

And then, blessedly, he was where he wanted to be. His Christmas wish. Flat on his back under the Christmas tree, with his wife astride him, her hair mussed and her mouth looking as if she'd been thoroughly kissed and her eyes glittering with desire.

He eased into her and his vision blurred; he wasn't sure whether he was seeing stars, the glow of the lights on the tree, or what. All he was aware of was her warm, wet heat wrapped round him. Of her fingers laced through his, tightening as her pleasure rose. Of her breathing growing faster and more shallow. Of the pleasure that gathered like a knot inside him, growing tighter and tighter and tighter until the final release. Of Kerry's name being dragged from his lips, and her answering cry. Of sitting up and wrapping his arms tightly round her as if he'd never, ever let her go again, her face buried in his shoulder and his face buried in her hair.

It was a long, long time until he came back down to earth. And then he realised that there were goosebumps on Kerry's skin. Cross with himself for not taking better care of her, he grabbed the nearest item of clothing—which turned out to be his shirt—and settled it round her shoulders. Drew her closer against his body so he could warm her with his body heat.

She resisted. 'I should go.'

'Why?'

'I… You're on shift tomorrow.'

'Tomorrow's another day.' He stroked her hair back from her forehead. 'Don't go. Stay with me tonight.'

Longing flickered into her face. Swiftly followed by cool reason. And then she opened her mouth to speak.

Adam didn't give her the chance to say no. He kissed her. Not hard, not roughly. Soft and sweet, his mouth just brushing the word away from her lips before he could hear it. And then she was matching him kiss for kiss, caress for caress. And she made no protest when he got to his feet, drawing her up with him. Didn't push him away when he picked her up, cradled her in his arms the same way he had when he'd carried her over the threshold of their honeymoon suite, and carried her to his bed.

* * *

Kerry woke early the next morning. Adam was still asleep, sprawled across the bed.

Her heart ached. How easy it would be to wake him with a kiss. Let the heat flare between them again so they took each other to paradise and back.

But that would make it even harder to say goodbye. And she wasn't going to cling. Wasn't going to beg him to change his ways for her, let her be his love for the rest of his life.

So she slipped quietly out of bed without waking him. Closed the door silently behind her. Untangled her clothes from his on the living room floor and dressed swiftly. Tidied the worst of the mess as silently as she could. Scrawled a note explaining that she had to go, and left it propped against the kettle. Then left Adam's flat before he woke. Before she could see the regret in his face.

CHAPTER SEVENTEEN

THE alarm beeped, jolting Adam from sleep.

Early shift.

Normally, he'd be awake before his alarm—but today was different. It was the morning after he'd spent the night making love with Kerry. And he really didn't want to get up.

Another five minutes wouldn't hurt.

Adam reached out and hit the snooze button, stretched, and rolled over to gather his wife into his arms, still with his eyes shut.

Except she wasn't there. And her side of the bed was freezing cold.

Which meant she'd been gone for quite a while.

Sighing inwardly, he opened his eyes. He'd been so sure that last night had been a breakthrough. That they were both finally ready to admit how they felt about each other.

But she'd fled.

What was she so scared of? That he'd abandon her, the way her parents had? Or that she'd follow in their footsteps and abandon him?

Both ideas were crazy.

Or maybe he was overreacting, fearing the worst when it

was nothing of the kind. Maybe she was in the bathroom, having a shower.

Ah, who was he trying to kid? She'd gone, all right. Without so much as a note. Unless she'd left him a note somewhere else.

He needed coffee.

Now.

He climbed out of bed and headed for the kitchen. She'd tidied the living room, he noticed—and the kitchen. Well, Kerry would. She was a neat freak.

And he saw the note propped against the kettle. 'Had to go. Display to set up. See you later.'

No specific time or date. Just 'later'.

Which meant she was really running scared.

How was he going to get through to her?

For a crazy moment, he thought about letting himself into her flat. Filling it with roses, spelling I Love You in chocolates on her kitchen table, setting her a puzzle to solve that would end up with the letters IELOOUVY which she'd have to rearrange to spell a three-word phrase…

But that wasn't Kerry's style. And she'd resent him for invading her space without invitation.

Somehow, he had to make her realise that he was serious about her. She'd been the only one he'd even considered as his fake fiancée, because he'd thought she was safe. Or maybe he'd been kidding himself all along: maybe he'd asked her because deep down she'd been the only one he'd wanted as his fiancée.

And he wanted her for real.

Saying 'I love you' wouldn't be enough. With her past, Kerry wouldn't believe it. Wouldn't dare to let herself believe it, in case she got hurt again. So there was only one thing he could think of that might convince her that he meant it.

Something outrageous.

Something that could get his heart broken very publicly.

It was a huge risk—but it was a risk he was prepared to take.

He glanced at the clock. Although his parents were larks rather than owls, it was still too early to call them. OK. Plan A: shower, breakfast, and call them on his way to the hospital.

He turned the temperature gauge in the shower until the water was as hot as he could bear it, to drown out the disappointment of not waking with Kerry in his arms. Not having breakfast in bed with her. Not sharing a shower before he left for his shift.

Last night had been perfect. So perfect. He'd told her how he felt, with every movement of his body. But clearly it hadn't been enough.

He forced down a mug of coffee and a couple of slices of toast, then glanced at his watch. Time for plan A.

His mother answered almost immediately. 'Moira McRae.'

'Hi, Mum. Happy Boxing Day. You and Dad OK?'

'Fine—just as we were when we spoke to you yesterday.' Moira sounded slightly anxious. 'Is everything all right, Adam?'

'Yes.' Well, no—but he hoped it was going to be. 'I'm just on my way to work. Can I ask you a huge favour, Mum?'

'Of course you can.'

'I need the phone number of whoever's in charge of the Inveraillie Hogmanay celebrations.'

'Why?'

'Can't tell you. It's a surprise for Kerry.' He took a deep breath. 'But it's important, Mum.' Really important. He might be doing the right thing, or he might be making the most spectacular mess of his life.

He just hoped it was the former.

'All right. Wait a second.' He heard paper rustling; clearly his mother was going through her address book. 'Got a pen?'

'Yup.' And the back of his hand would do nicely as something to write on.

He wrote down the name and number she gave him. 'Thanks, Mum. I'll see you soon.'

'Love you, Adam.'

Something she always said to him, and he always mumbled something uncontroversial. So he said something he knew he should have said a lot more often. 'Love you too, Mum.' He cleared the line and dialled the number she'd just given him. And, after a fairly involved conversation, it was all set up.

He just had to pray this would work.

Kerry had the best possible excuse to avoid Adam before New Year's Eve: she was busy sorting out last-minute glitches in the displays she'd designed, and briefing the people who were going to set them off to make sure that everything would go as planned.

And then it was time to leave for Scotland.

Scotland, and her last day with Adam.

She pushed the thought to the back of her mind and forced herself to smile. And at least Adam hadn't asked her why she'd left his flat so early on Boxing Day.

He was probably relieved she hadn't caused a scene, she realised. And it made her heart ache. How was she going to get through New Year's Eve? The celebrations were always such a big deal in Scotland. He'd be pretending he loved her, for his family's sake. And she'd be running a double bluff: pretending to him that she was only pretending to be in love with him.

It made her head ache, as well as her heart. She found

herself growing quieter and quieter on the way to Edinburgh, and quieter still as Adam drove them to Inveraillie.

'You OK?' he asked gently as they turned into the village.

No. She didn't belong here. Not really. And what they were doing was oh, so wrong. 'I'm fine,' she lied.

And then they were turning into the driveway of his parents' house. Moira and Donald had clearly been watching from the window, because they rushed out to greet them with hugs and kisses. Their welcome was genuine, and it broke Kerry's heart. This was the family she could have had. The family she'd always wanted.

But they weren't hers to keep.

Then Adam carried their bags to their room.

Their room.

Even the thought sent ripples of desire down her spine. Bittersweet ripples, because this was the last night she would share with Adam. The end of everything.

Moira made a fuss of them, and had clearly gone to a lot of trouble; the big farmhouse kitchen smelled of baking and there were lidded tins stacked neatly on the worktop—filled with cakes and cookies and Scots delicacies, Kerry was sure.

But the bit that almost broke her was when she sat next to Adam in the living room and noticed the framed wedding photograph on the mantelpiece. Herself and Adam, smiling out. As if she were really part of the family. Really belonged.

And how she wished…

Pointless. It wasn't going to happen. Tomorrow she'd be on a plane to LA.

And then people started dropping in. People who were delighted to meet the bride of the boy they had never thought would settle down. Even Elspeth MacAllister—the woman his parents had wanted him to marry—came in to wish them the best. And she was so sincere, Kerry could have cried. Didn't they all realise she was a fake?

Somehow she managed to get through dinner.

'I know it's a bit of a busman's holiday for you,' Moira said, 'but we always go to the village firework display at Hogmanay. I bought tickets for the four of us.'

'That'll be lovely,' Kerry said. 'It's always interesting to see what kind of things other designers do—and I just love the magic of fireworks anyway.'

And the magic of the fireworks between herself and Adam...

She shook herself. She was already on borrowed time. She'd had one night longer with him than she should have had. Broken his rules. No wonder he'd been slightly edgy with her today. Running scared.

The event was held on the local rugby club's playing field, and it looked as if half the neighbouring villages were there as well. She couldn't remember the names of everyone who came up to congratulate her and Adam on their marriage, and her face ached with smiling by the time the display started.

'I've got a bit of a headache,' she said quietly to Adam. 'D'you think anyone would mind if I slipped back to your parents' place?'

'It's not a huge display. About fifteen minutes, I'd guess,' Adam said. 'I promise I'll take you straight back to Mum and Dad's afterwards, if you want. Just stay for this bit. Please?'

He had a point. If she left now, people would start to wonder what was wrong. Might even guess at the truth—a truth that would be devastating to Donald and Moira. That wasn't the way it was supposed to happen: she'd just fade out of his life and he'd tell his parents he'd made a mistake, rushed into things, and they weren't right for each other.

So she agreed to stay. Promised herself she'd act her part

perfectly. And she tried not to flinch when he put his arm round her shoulders. People always expected newlyweds to be demonstrative, didn't they?

With her professional hat on, she judged it a fair display. There was a good mix of colours and effects, and the audience seemed captivated.

No Catherine wheels, though, she noticed. Pity. They were one of her favourites.

There was a volley of starbursts, but just when she thought the display was over, Adam moved to stand behind her. Let his arm drop from her shoulder so he could slide it round her waist, and pulled her back against him. '*This* is why I wanted you to stay,' he said. 'For the finale.'

The finale? She frowned. Hadn't they already had that?

And then she saw the display fizzing at the bottom of the field. The Catherine wheels she'd thought were missing. And they spelled out a message: A ♥ K.

She blinked hard. Stared at the display again. And it still said the same thing. A ♥ K.

Adam loves Kerry.

'Does that say...?' she began, her voice shaky. 'Your parents organised this?'

'No. I did,' he said.

For his parents' sake. Right. She could understand that.

But then he drew her closer still. 'I've been trying to tell you for a while,' he whispered against her ear. 'And this was the only way I could think of to make you listen.'

Telling her he loved her—in fireworks.

Fireworks. The same fizzy, buzzy feeling that was currently shimmering throughout her entire body.

'I love you, Kerry,' Adam said. 'I think I've loved you for a long time. I was just too scared to admit that I'm just like everyone else—that I wanted one special person in my life.

That I wanted to settle down.' He brushed his lips against her earlobe. 'That I wanted one person in particular. You.'

'But I thought…this was all meant to be…' For his parents' benefit. To make them happy, make them think that Adam had finally settled down.

'It was. At first. But then I realised what I really feel about you. I told you on our wedding day.'

They'd made love, yes—but she couldn't remember him saying, 'I love you.'

As if he guessed what she was thinking, he asked, 'Remember you asked me what I said to you before I lifted your veil?'

'Uh-huh.'

He repeated the words softly. *'Aon bhodhaig, le cheile bhon là seo a-mach, Aon anam aonaicte, gun sgaradh a chaoidh, Cridhe mo chridhesa, bheir mi dhut mo ghaol, Dean mar a thogras tu leis.'*

'I don't speak Gaelic,' she said, equally softly.

'I'll translate it for you. One body together from this day forward. One soul united never to be parted. Heart of my heart, I give you my love. Do with it as you will.'

The words sank in.

Heart of my heart, I give you my love.

She turned to face him. Children nearby were waving fibre-optic torches around, and the light was enough to show her his face. To show her his sincerity.

He meant it.

'You love me,' she said in wonder.

'With all my heart,' he said. 'I know you have issues—that you've been let down before. That you saw your mother let down. That it's hard for you to trust. But we're not your parents. And I have a good example to follow—my parents have been married for thirty-five years and they're still going strong.' He stroked her face. 'Our marriage can work. *Will* work. Because I love you.'

'But…you have the biggest little black book in London.'

'Had,' he corrected. 'I haven't even looked at another woman since the day I put that green sapphire on your ring finger. Since the day I asked you to be my fiancée. I've turned down every single offer made to me—because nobody matches up to you. *Nobody*,' he emphasised.

'I thought you'd just oiled your bedsprings so I couldn't hear you,' she muttered.

He shook his head, sliding his hands back down to span her waist. 'You must be joking. There's only one woman I want to share my bed. The one who holds my heart. The one who's in my arms right now. My wife. And I want to make our marriage a proper one.'

Dared she believe it?

For a moment, the dream shimmered.

And then it broke. 'Adam… I signed a contract. My new job. I have to go to LA.'

He shrugged. 'It's not for ever. Just for a while. Maybe I can get leave and come with you. And if it turns out to be the job of your heart, what you really want to do, there are always exchange programmes between hospitals. I can get a job near where you work. We can sort something out. Just as long as we're together.' He paused. 'That is, if you love me?'

He had to ask? Kerry stared at him. 'But…don't you know?'

He shook his head. 'When I got that set of photos from Trish, I saw one you didn't show me. One where it was so obvious I loved you, from the look on my face. I thought you'd taken it out because you'd realised and you didn't feel the same.'

'More like, that photograph showed that I was in love with you, and I didn't think you felt the same so I didn't want you to see it and be embarrassed,' she corrected.

'I can't believe we've been such idiots,' he said. 'All the time we've wasted, when we could h—'

She pressed her forefinger to his lips. 'Not wasted. Maybe we weren't quite ready. It's a hell of a step, from keeping people at a distance to opening your heart. Making yourself vulnerable.'

'Yeah. For both of us. Me with my no-commitment rule, wanting to be the one to end it so I didn't get hurt. And you were the same.' He took a deep breath. 'But I've known for a long time that I trust you more than anyone else on earth. You're the only one I ever talked to about anything important, right from when I first met you and fed you chocolate biscuits. Nobody else would do.' He dipped his head and brushed his mouth against hers. 'And for me, love and trust are the same. I love you, Kerry. I trust you. *Cridhe mo chridhesa, bheir mi dhut mo ghaol.*'

'Heart of my heart,' Kerry said softly. 'I had no idea what you were saying to me then. But when I made my wedding vows…they were for real. I love you, Adam.'

He wrapped his arms round her, holding her tightly. 'Good. But you know what this means, don't you?'

'What?'

'The pairs thing. Adam loves Kerry.' He dropped a kiss on the end of her nose. 'I'm going to have to admit you're right. It's alpha order.'

'And Kerry loves Adam. You're right, too. Not alpha order,' she said with a smile.

'Today's the end of the year,' he said. 'The end of the old. The start of the new. The start of our marriage. And you'll wake every day from now on knowing that I love you.'

'That we love each other,' Kerry corrected softly.

The Catherine wheels were still fizzing.

'They'll burn out,' Adam said, holding her close, 'but our love won't. And even if we have to be apart for a while, it won't stop me loving you.'

'Or me loving you.' And she knew she'd finally found the one she was looking for. The man who understood her. Who loved her. And who told her…with fireworks.

researching the cure

The facts you need to know:

- Breast cancer is the commonest form of cancer in the United Kingdom. **One woman in nine** will develop the disease during her lifetime.

- Each year around **41,000** women and approximately **300** men are diagnosed with breast cancer and around **13,000** women and **90** men will die from the disease.

- 80% of all breast cancers occur in post-menopausal women and approximately 8,200 pre-menopausal women are diagnosed with the disease each year.

- However, survival rates are improving, with on average 77.5% of women diagnosed between 1996 and 1999 still alive five years later, compared to 72.8% for women diagnosed between 1991 and 1996.

Breast Cancer Campaign is the only charity that specialises in funding independent breast cancer research throughout the UK. It aims to find the cure for breast cancer by funding research which looks at improving diagnosis and treatment of breast cancer, better understanding how it develops and ultimately either curing the disease or preventing it.

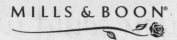

All you could want for Christmas!

Meet handsome and seductive men under the mistletoe, escape to the world of Regency romance or simply relax by the fire with a heartwarming tale by one of our bestselling authors. These special stories will fill your holiday with Christmas sparkle!

On sale 6th October 2006

On sale 20th October 2006